THE BOOK OF THE MAD

TANITH LEE

THE BOOK OF THE MAD

THE SECRET BOOKS OF PARADYS · IV

THE OVERLOOK PRESS
WOODSTOCK, NEW YORK

First published in 1993 by
The Overlook Press
Lewis Hollow Road
Woodstock, New York 12498

Library of Congress Cataloging-in-Publication Data

Lee, Tanith.

    The book of the mad / Tanith Lee.
       p. cm. —(The Secret books of Paradys ; 4)
    I. Title   II. Series : Lee, Tanith. Secret books of Paradys ; 4.
PR6062.E4163B675   1993
823'.914—dc20   92-36788
                                                       CIP
ISBN: 0-87951-481-7

Typeset by AeroType, Inc.

Tired moons ask higher tides.

Zelda Fitzgerald

LE LIVRE ORANGE

Paradise

▲

The sun shall not smite thee by day,
nor the moon by night.

Psalms

It was early afternoon, but as ever the daytime City was enveloped in gray mist. The sun had been invisible for years. The architecture of the City itself—decayed, ruinous, romantic, and depressing by turns—was visible in shifting patches, or regularly to a distance of seven meters. So that, as Felion climbed the long stair of a hundred steps, his world sank away into a sea of fog from which a few ghostly towers poked. And above, the Terrace of Birds began to form around a single dot of light—which would be Smara's lamp. That is, he doubted anyone else would have climbed up here. The unhinged citizens of Paradise were also sluggish and indifferent, obsessed with rituals and trivia.

Felion stepped off onto the terrace. Through the mist, the strange dim stone figures of bird-headed things perched on the balustrade, their long beaks moistly shining. In their midst, the amber lamp floated obediently in the air. Smara stood beneath it. Slim and blond as Felion, and wrapped in a sleek, pale dress, she stared at him with essential recognition. They were twins.

"I haven't seen you for a week," he said. "How are you?"

"Sane," said Smara. "And you?"

Felion laughed. "We two," he said.

He went over to her, took her hand, and laid it against

9

his face. He loved her, but in the wrong way. Brother and sister, they were expected by their society to be incestuous, it was the custom. But then the customs of Paradise were wild and sometimes uncouth. The polluted chemical saturation of the atmosphere, which produced the eternal mists of Paradise and eroded the buildings, had influenced the minds that lived there. For some reason, Felion and Smara were not mad, at least not in the accepted manner. They had therefore no friends, no lovers. They had had an uncle, but he was gone. Nevertheless, he was their reason for meeting at this place, for climbing up the hundred steps to his tilted mansion on the City tops.

"Do you remember when he brought us here?" asked Felion of Smara. "These bird statues frightened you."

"That was your fault," said Smara, "and you made it worse."

"So I did. But you were the only one I had power over. We were just children."

"I know why you wanted to come here," she said. "But I'm not really willing. Don't you think, after all, it would be an act of madness?"

"Perhaps. Isn't that good?"

Smara looked away, down across the City. From the denser lower levels of the fog, the decayed towers of the cathedral rose. "Today it's quite easy to see, the Temple-Church."

"Yes. But tomorrow it may be hidden."

"Don't you think," she said, "our uncle might have lied? We were children, as you said. I barely recollect what we saw."

"I've never forgotten. I've dreamed of it for years. That wall of smoking *whiteness*—"

"No," she said. "No, don't."

"You must help me," he said.

"Why? If it *is* a labyrinth, it's simple. One hand always on the left side wall, and it will bring you to the center. And the right side wall to return."

"Then you don't want to come with me to see—"

10

"Maybe it goes nowhere. Why should it go anywhere? He was mad, too."

Felion gazed up at the bird things. He said slowly, "He named us as his heirs. That was straightforward enough. So we inherit this pile of stone, and we inherit the labyrinth, if it exists—and it does. And then there's that rambling letter he wrote to us. The *rest* of the inheritance."

"Suppose," she said, "you and I are insane, like all of them. But we haven't realized."

He shrugged. She did not look alarmed—even, possibly, hopeful.

"We've done our best to act out madness," he said. "What else can we do?" He took her hand again. "Let's go in. Let's see what the house is like, at least."

They went over the terrace to the big door, and Felion spoke to it the numbers written in their uncle's parting letter. The door opened, and a long dark hall stretched out, lined with marble abstracts, ending in a broad stair. High up, a round window let in the sinister light. Mist hung on the air.

They walked in, and for two hours they went over the mansion their uncle had willed to them. It was like every-where else, no better, no worse, one with the other grand and rotting buildings of the City, bulging with furniture, art objects, defaced books, and technological gadgets, which, usually, had ceased to function.

Finally they came down into the basement, and there they found the narrow door that neither of them, in fact, had forgotten.

"Shall we see if it's still there? Perhaps it's vanished."

He told off the other set of numbers to the door, and when it swung away, he moved down the sloping floor beyond. After a moment, Smara followed him.

At the bottom, in blackness but for the glow of Smara's floating lamp, was the odd little railway track and the car-riage that ran along it. But the car refused to work. So then they walked along the track, between the blank walls, and so out into a kind of cavern, which must lie somewhere inside

11

the hill, behind the hundred steps, and under the foundations of deserted houses.

At the far end of the cavern rose a white gleaming wetness.

It was another wall, but it seemed made, of all things, from ice. An arched entry led into it. Inside, only more of the whiteness was to be seen.

"Of course," he said, "it would have scared you. You were afraid of winter, even though there never is a winter anymore."

"It was the picture you showed me on that screen. The snowfields, and the frozen water."

"But this," he said, "how can it be ice?"

"It could be anything," she said quietly. "*He* made it."

Their gnarled uncle had claimed to be a scientist, a physicist and mathematician. That one day in childhood when he had brought them to his house, he had explained to them so many things that they had understood nothing at all. And then he showed them this.

It was a labyrinth, he said, built by him, that formed a connection between two worlds: the world of Paradise and the world of another city, similar but also different. In this other city the atmosphere was clear, a sun and a moon and stars shone down. Technologically, its society was not so advanced, but neither had it atrophied. And while an aspect of madness prevailed there, it was not the rooted insanity of Paradise.

"I believe," said Felion, "that he did what he said. He reached the second city and he lived there. And as he approached death, he decided to offer us, too, the chance of freedom."

"How spiteful of him," she said, "to make us wait so long."

"But time is changeable in the labyrinth, didn't he say so? We could penetrate this world at any point in time, past, future—I don't grasp the ethic of it. It must be random, uncontrollable."

"Or a lie," she said again.

12

"But he was gone for years," said Felion. "Where did he go?"

"Oh, he concealed himself."

The white wall remained there before them, empty, menacing; unavoidable?

Smara moved away, and began to return along the track in the floor. Presently Felion went after her.

They negotiated the slope and emerged from the door, which shut, back into the basement.

"Did you," she said, "kill this week?"

"Oh, twice," he said. "An old woman on the river bank, and a painter near the cathedral. I saved you his brushes."

"I haven't killed," she said. "So I must. I'll do it tonight."

"Shall I come with you?" he asked, solicitously, gently.

"I prefer to work alone when I can. But thank you. Shall we meet at the bar beside the third broken bridge? I'll kill someone with rings, and bring you one, Felion."

ONE

Paradis

●

There was a little girl
Who had a little curl
Right in the middle of her forehead;
And when she was good
She was very, very good,
And when she was bad she was horrid.

—Longfellow

After the storm the wrecked ship lay on the beach, against the bright broken gray of the sea. From the ship's side spilled her cargo of smashed glass and oranges, like blood from a wound. Her sail hung, a snapped wing. In the sky, great white clouds massed.

Leocadia stepped back from the painting and put down her brush. She rubbed her hands on a rag.

Was the picture finished? Yes. Surely. And yet...

Perhaps there should be a figure, hanged, depending from the ruined mast, with long black curling hair.

If she painted that into the picture, it would help them, would it not? Of course, they would say, because she is insane, she paints herself hanged from the ship's mast.

Leocadia shook back her long black curling hair, which fell almost to her waist. Her features were sharply clear as porcelain, and out of her feline face looked two black eyes. She had been admired before, and she had lost count of her lovers, of both sexes, only recalling a few with nostalgia or irritation.

There had always been enough money to do as she wished. To drink and fornicate and paint. She had never envisaged anything else, except perhaps one day a novel she would write, a lover who might truly pleasure or pain her, the possibility that alcohol might undo her. But not yet. She was thirty. Her parents, who had died when she was five, in a car accident on one of the vast new City highways, would normally have lived long. Life expectancy was quite high, and her family, especially its women, survived. There had been the two grandmothers—thin, healthy, wicked old women, vaguely resembling each other—one with hair that, at a hundred and three, was still thick with jet black waves. But the grandmothers were gone now, and the uncle, her guardian, had died in the winter (no one was invited to the funeral) at ninety years of age. He was incredibly, frightfully, frighteningly rich. That had never mattered. Then it turned out that it did.

Leocadia went into the little alcove, and opened the refrigerator. She took out a bottle of white transparent wine and uncorked it. The cold box was full of the things she liked, salads and cheeses, smoked fish, drink. She wanted for nothing. (They saw to that—was it their guilt?) Nothing but that amorphous element, her freedom.

"Imprisoned, poor thing." Leocadia spoke to the wine in the bottle. "Let me set you at liberty."

Her cousin, Nanice, had arrived at ten, on that morning in the past. She had not been alone. The man might have been taken for an escort, a boyfriend. Nanice was ugly, but she too had money. And anyway, the man was ugly also. They stood, uglily, on the steps below the old house which had, nevertheless, been fitted with an automatic door. The door relayed their images to the bedroom, where Leocadia was lying in the sheets with Asra.

Leocadia slept with women more from a wish for power than from lust. She loved their lips and breasts, but mostly she liked their helpless pleasure, and that they would tend to defer to her. Asra, though, was pert.

"Good God, who are those awful creatures?" said Asra.

"I don't know." And Leocadia had touched the intercom. "Who are you?" she asked.

"I am your cousin, Nanice le Vey. And this is Monsieur Saume. May we come in?"

"Lock the doors, load the cannon!" cried Asra.

"It's a little early," said Leocadia. She had felt nothing but mildly annoyed. No premonition.

"It's after ten," Nanice had said with strange smugness. "And we've come such a long way."

"Why?" said Leocadia.

"Do you mean to be uncivil?"

"Probably."

"If we must, we'll wait elsewhere, and return later."

"I repeat, why?"

Nanice preened herself, the redundant gesture of a well-but-ill-dressed, unattractive person.

"It's about Uncle Michelot."

"He's dead."

Nanice frowned. "Yes, I know the poor old gentleman is deceased."

The images from the door were incoming only, and Leocadia rose naked from her bed. Yet Nanice seemed to sense this, and she frowned more heavily.

"I will let you in," said Leocadia. "Wait in the salon downstairs. The service will bring you anything you want."

It came to Leocadia that the salon, which was often quite tidy, dusted by the house service, and the floor polished, accented by fresh flowers, was on that day disheveled. The previous evening she had allowed Asra to have a sort of party, and the service had not yet been summoned to clear up the mess. The ashtrays overflowed with the stubs of cigarishis, the pictures were crooked, bottles and books lay everywhere, the light was still on, and someone, probably Robert, had been sick in a vase.

Leocadia laughed. She visualized the stiff visitors in the midst of chaos as she went to the shower. Asra lay in bed, complaining: She hated people, they had had enough of people the night before. Leocadia, who had been stupid enough to have relatives, must make them go away.

Leocadia went down half an hour later to the salon. She wore a cream silk housedress, her hair was wet, and she was barefoot. In one hand she bore a tangerine, which she was eating, flesh and peel and pips together, and in the other a tall glass of white vodka.

The visitors were perched in the midst of chaos, as anticipated. Monsieur Saume stood, his hat in his hand, and Nanice teetered on a chair as if afraid it must be dirtying her skirt.

The room smelled thickly of smoke and drugs and perfume, thankfully not of vomit.

Leocadia pressed a button and the windows opened.

Outside, the spring day was warm yet brisk, and the gray streets of old Paradis curved and climbed among the ancient plane trees.

"So," said Nanice, "this is how you live."

She looked happy, and quickly smoothed her expression back to one of discomfiture.

Leocadia curled her toes about a black bottle lying on the rug, and picked up the glass with her foot.

"Yes, luckily you came at a quiet time."

"Quiet! My dear Leocadia—what are you doing to yourself!" exclaimed Nanice. Her protestation was so insincere, that even Monsieur Saume seemed embarrassed.

"I am," said Leocadia, "existing."

"And there is," said Nanice to Monsieur Saume, "a young woman in the bedroom, as you heard. And in that glass—don't *think* it's water."

"Would you like a vodka?" asked Leocadia. "I suppose you'd prefer something less pure; tea or coffee, I expect."

"No, nothing, thank you," said Nanice.

"Then perhaps you'd tell me, at last, why you are here."

Nanice lowered her eyes.

Her falseness was so utter, so unflawed, that Leocadia was fascinated.

"You have no guardian, now Uncle Michelot has died. I know," said Nanice, "you haven't seen him, been near him, for years—"

18

"No one has," said Leocadia. "He was a recluse. He disliked intrusion. One wonders why."

"Oh, I tried to see him," said Nanice. "One *could* try. Cousin Brand and I were constantly making approaches. But as you say, either he was a very private man, or else ..." Nanice looked momentarily laughably cunning, as if she could hardly credit how clever she was being. "Or else someone put him against us. Against all of us."

Leocadia shrugged. From her uncle and former guardian she had received adequate funds, and once a year, on her name day, she had been sent some gift, always simple, never very expensive, but infallibly strange. The news of his death had jarred Leocadia. She had scanned the letter bordered in black, slightly puzzled by its wording, which seemed to say, euphemistically, that he had gone to better things. The letter told her, too, that Michelot had made provision for her, and she was glad of that. She had never known him, beyond a glimpse or two in childhood. He had chuckled, apparently, when she was expelled from her school, and provided her with private tuition. He seemed to understand her well enough, and did not insult her with feigned affection.

Nanice, of course, would have wanted much more. Family gatherings of hugs and kisses, rich presents, and now, obviously, some remuneration that was, presumably, absent?

"He left you out of his will?" asked Leocadia, pouring more vodka and ice into her glass from the entering service tray, and from a silver pot a cup of delicate, slaty tea.

"His—oh, Leocadia. You know quite well that he left out all of us. This wasn't what I came here to discuss, but if you insist. All twenty-three of his nearest and dearest were discounted. His kindred. All but you, and—well, this is very odd—two other cousins no one has heard of and who cannot be traced. They are mentioned as *your* inheritators. But frankly, we think he *made them up*."

"Oh dear," said Leocadia. "Is that why Monsieur Saume is with you? In case I've been invented too?"

19

Nanice looked abruptly flustered.

"Monsieur Saume is—my companion."

"And he has no tongue," said Leocadia. "What a shame. A man's tongue has so many wonderful uses."

Nanice stared. Then she colored. Monsieur Saume did not alter. He had not moved at all, like a skillful lizard on a rock when predators are nearby.

Leocadia took a sip of tea, then a sip of vodka, and let the bottle drop from her toes.

"I still don't see what you want from me. Are you asking me to make you some sort of bequest? I will if you like, but your own lawyers must see to it. Such matters are very boring. I have things I like to do instead."

"Paint horrible nightmarish pictures and sleep with lesbians!" cried Nanice in an explosion of true venom. "And drink your brains to slop. Oh, I know. We've been watching you—"

"Mademoiselle le Vey," said Monsieur Saume.

Leocadia was surprised. At the final response of the silent Saume. And at the idea that someone had been watching her. It was true, Leocadia was used to being stared at: She was both striking and eccentric and did not much care what she did before others. But to be the object of a spy?

"Why have you watched me?"

Nanice compressed her little mouth into a littler line, like a zip.

It was Monsieur Saume who said, "There has been some concern, mademoiselle."

Leocadia raised her eyebrows.

"Well, it can stop now. As you see. Here I am."

"It can hardly stop," said Nanice. The zip wriggled vindictively. Again, Nanice seemed happy.

"But I," said Leocadia, "say it *must* stop."

And as others had done, confronted by Leocadia's anger, Nanice looked alarmed.

"Monsieur Saume," she cried, "you see she's quite unstable, like her paintings we showed you—"

There had been a recent exhibition of Leocadia's work at the First Gallery on Clock Tower Hill. Some pieces had been sold for quite extravagant amounts of cash. Did Nanice resent this, too?

Refilling her glass of white wine now, in the alcove of the refrigerator, Leocadia understood quite well that Nanice had wanted Monsieur Saume and others like him to note the content of the pictures, not their cost. The centaurs with the heads of swordfish, the horses in ballgowns, the women in the arms of women, men in the arms of men, winged cats and burning mansions.

But then, that day in the salon of the old house near the antique City wall, Leocadia had lost patience, and so rendered Nanice invaluable assistance.

"I'm afraid," said Leocadia, "you must get out. You're wasting my time. If I lay eyes on you again, Nanice le Vey, I'll have you thrown, down, off something, into the river. Do I make myself clear?"

Nanice sprang up. And her look now was of real terror mixed with great satisfaction. As she moved toward the door she knocked into the vase Robert had used, which broke on the floor, splattering her with sick and dead ferns.

Monsieur Saume, hat in hand, bowed to Leocadia before he effected his leave. She might have guessed from that, and maybe she partly did, that he had taken an interest in her.

The doctors came at five o'clock (seventeen hours, by the old, unfashionable time scale). Sometimes there were two, sometimes three or four doctors. There were no women among them, and Leocadia had long suspected that this was due to some notion that she would be able to seduce and subvert a woman more easily than a man. Or perhaps because all the men were hideous.

Sometimes even Saume came to see her.

They never stayed long, nor did they arrive every day. She never knew when they would come. Possibly this was meant to disorient, but it only irritated her.

Frequently, she took no notice of them, but now and again they played tricks.

One brought a cat, which Leocadia saw was clockwork. Even so she had liked it, and when they were all, apparently, sure of that, they bore it away and never brought it back. She was not allowed animals. She might "hurt" them. Leocadia explained that it was human things she disliked.

Another time a doctor had left her an orange. When she experimentally peeled it, it bled.

So now she kept an eye on the doctors when they appeared in her apartment.

"Mademoiselle. How are you today?"

"Anxious to leave."

"Ah," playfully, "*mademoiselle.*"

They—there were now two of them, Saume and Van Orles—advanced on her painting.

"It's finished." They stared at the wrecked ship.

"Perhaps," she said.

"And what does this represent?"

"What do you think?" said Leocadia.

"A broken heart?" inquired Doctor Van Orles lubriciously, leering at her.

"No," said Leocadia. "Have you considered glasses or lenses for your eyes?"

Van Orles laughed. "Now, now, Leocadia."

"A ship," said Saume.

"Well done," said Leocadia. "A ship run aground."

"Oranges?" asked Van Orles. "Why is that?"

"Why not?" said Leocadia.

"There has been a storm," Van Orles explained to her carefully. "And the cargo has been lost."

"As I have lost my mind? I'm not," said Leocadia, "full of oranges."

"But of broken glass?" asked Saume.

"You're rather ignorant," said Leocadia. "The ancient ships carried smashed glass for recycling."

"Are there monkeys?" pressed Van Orles. "Perhaps the captain kept some." He seemed excited by the painting.

"Give me a model," said Leocadia, "a monkey to pose. I'll add a couple."

"And how much have you drunk today, Leocadia?" asked Van Orles.

Leocadia looked at him. "I don't count."

"But you *should* count, Leocadia. This is so bad for your health."

"All the better, I'd have thought. Maybe I'll die, and then the cousins won't have to pay for my place here. One less annoying little expense."

She had wondered, at first, if they might poison her, and of course they did, but only in subtle ways that would not be disallowed. Beams of light that penetrated the brain, and sounds she could not, or could barely, hear. Some nights, all through the dark, a slender bell chimed far away.

The walls of the room were a pale, soft dove color, restful, but against them, when her eyes were tired, she saw things in the fluid of her sight, disturbing and worrying, which, against a jumble of objects, textures, and colors, would not have been visible.

They destroyed her, inch by inch. Meter by meter. But she would not be destroyed. She must rebuild what was chipped away.

"There are no figures at all in your painting," said Van Orles.

"Alas," said Leocadia.

"Should you care for visitors?"

"Visitors put me here."

"Surely there's someone you would like to see?"

"I'd tell them how you torture me."

"Now, Mademoiselle. You're thinking of terrible crimes of the past. The *old* asylum. You mustn't dwell on that."

"There are drugs in my food. Unseen lights and unheard noises crisscross this room. I'm kept so docile."

"*You?* Mademoiselle, you? *Docile?*"

"You sedate me," said Leocadia, offhand. "How else is it I don't fly at you with my palette knife, my fork, the file for my nails?"

"Because you are civilized," said Saume, "and you don't

23

wish to sully your art, your food, or your person by an artifact used in murder against, merely, us."

She regarded him. He was sometimes quaint and caught her attention.

"I shall need another canvas," said Leocadia.

"Oh, yes," said Van Orles. "It will be arranged. Everything for your happiness."

"Then let me out."

"Oh. Dear mademoiselle."

A week after the advent of Nanice at the house, Leocadia had forgotten her.

Asra, in an effort to energize Leocadia, had taken up with another woman, and Leocadia was quite pleased, getting her house to herself without the effort of making a scene. She intended to remove Asra's code from the automatic door, but she gradually forgot this, too.

One afternoon, Saume called. She would not have let him in, but she had been out walking in the park under the Roman wall, staring at the remains of gravestones left standing in the grass, and the sides of demolished houses up which ivy had been trained. She found Saume on her steps.

"Yes?"

"I am here to see you, mademoiselle."

"I'm afraid you're mistaken."

"I beg your pardon."

"I am going to go in, and you are not."

Saume only smiled—he had dreadful teeth, like something medieval, for generally teeth now were universally excellent.

He held out a slender book.

"You wish me to sign it?" asked Leocadia, for it was her collection, the only one, of short stories.

"I am simply intrigued by the content. Girls who turn into vampire owls. Raccoons who romantically subdue their jailers in prison and tickle ladies with their stripy tails. Where does your inspiration come from?"

"The City," said Leocadia. "These are old stories of Paradis."

"Indeed? I haven't come across them."

"Goodbye," said Leocadia.

She went in and shut the door in his face. He did not attempt to intrude further. Just then.

Summer came, and Leocadia lay under a white sunshade in her overgrown garden, which she had planted to a kind of jungle. Sometimes Asra called her, but Leocadia was non-committal. She was in a phase when she was more than content to be alone, not realizing that soon this was to become a permanent arrangement.

Her house was supposed to be haunted. Robert said he had seen someone walk out of a wall. Many of the houses near the old wall were reckoned to have a psychic persuasion.

Leocadia painted a ghost standing on a rooftop, looking lost and slightly belligerent.

But when she had finished a painting, generally Leocadia grew a little restless. She had finished one. Now it was a landscape with dancing figures, lit by far high hills in sunset, pumpkin-colored, radiating heat and menace.

Leocadia dressed in a long, pale beaded frock, preparing to go out and dine in the City. And as if on cue, Pir called her. He asked, begged her to come to a dinner at the Surprise Restaurant. "So many people," said Pir. "Lots of champagne."

Leocadia decided she would go, because sometimes, at a painting's end, she liked to move among crowds, experiencing to the full her total difference from them.

Pir was eager and came to collect her in his long car, which moved slowly, as was the City habit now, save on the dangerous fast highways.

The Surprise lay on the lower bank, a block of bright buildings, perhaps (or not) erected on the sight of an old tavern. The river glimmered down below, and above the hills lifted from the City with their crowns of new and ancient architecture. The Temple-Church was floodlit, and owls nested in its upper galleries. No bells rang from it now—they had lost their voices—yet sometimes in sleep, Leocadia heard them.

The people of the crowd in the restaurant were stupid and drunken, already stuffing themselves with dishes of quail in jelly and black caviar. On the tables of the private room where the party went on were tall cones of treated meltless ice containing flowers.

Pir led Leocadia to a table. She sat down and drank a champagne which had too much head, like stomach salts.

"All the world says 'never,'" said Leocadia.

"What?" asked Pir.

"An old song. Everybody says 'never,' always 'never.'"

"I don't understand."

"None of them have anything to say, and all of them want to say it."

Pir grimaced.

"You're too clever for me. What will you eat, you beaded monster?"

Leocadia selected a dish from the menu.

Gradually people flooded around her. She found herself the center of an odd type of attention, bantering and fulsome, with undercurrents of insult.

Asra was not there, and presently Jacqueline Degot remarked on it. "She says she's afraid to be where you are, Leocadia. She says you terrify and intimidate her."

"Not noticeably," said Leocadia, who was finding the food rather bland.

"But yes." Jacqueline was insistent. She was clad as a huge blond nymph. "Asra says you have frightened her so much she can't go anywhere near you."

"And yet," added Pir, "one can see she *longs* to do exactly that. Can't you relent, Leocadia?"

Leocadia found this incomprehensible and did not bother to reply. An idea for a short poem was beginning to come into her head. She realized the dinner was ghastly. Inebriated women already lay over the tables, with tiddly men

26

nibbling grapes from their cleavages, and elsewhere. The waiters came and went like well-behaved penguins. Which was foolish, for surely no penguin would ever be so idiotic.

Leocadia considered penguins. She must visit the zoological gardens of Paradis.

"And Asra complains," added Claude Ful, "that you've treated her roughly. That you struck her."

Leocadia took no notice of this either. For some reason the image of penguins had taken hold of her, or rather of one especial penguin, a nun of feathers, upright and perfect on a raft of ice. . . .

She rose to her feet.

"No, no," cried Pir, "you mustn't leave yet."

"But I must."

"Stay—at least until midnight."

"Certainly not."

Pir pushed against Leocadia, trying to refill her glass and grab her arm.

Normally people had learned not to treat her in this way. She thrust him back and he stumbled against a cavorting couple. "Oh! Oh! Don't be so violent, Leocadia."

"Then don't make me so violent."

Pir slipped aside, but others formed a garland around her. She went through them, and their gloved hands broke away, the sliding doors of their bodies slid.

"Stop her!" exclaimed Jacqueline, as if Leocadia were a thief who had snatched something.

Leocadia had never, since childhood—when she had vanquished it—felt fear. But now there was an unease that, in another, might have amounted to fear.

The dinner guests were swarming at her like a herd.

She plucked a silver knife from a table and held it up.

And the wall of flesh crumpled back with tiny sounds of disapproval and drunken laughter. "What's the matter with her? She acts as if we're the enemy."

At the door, three penguins (or waiters) let Leocadia pass without trouble. And she descended the noisy, lighted restaurant and went out.

She was on the street, the river flowing somewhere and the pure lamps of Paradis, which now never failed, shining upon her.

She walked idly, toward a bridge.

But something was happening. What was it? The new and the old areas of the City, rubbing their unliking flanks together; she had seen and moved through this before. Occasionally difficult persons might extrude themselves and attempt a woman on her own, but rarely, for the watching TV eyes of police surveillance were scattered about, and besides, Leocadia did not look a natural victim. Once when she was fifteen a mugger had come at her in an antique lane. She had punched him on the point of the jaw with her slim, steely hand, bruising the joints of her fingers but knocking him out. And now she had forgetfully kept the knife from the restaurant. Doubtless it would be best to throw that in the river, for a woman wandering Paradis by night with a table knife might also be suspect.

She was coming down toward the river, pausing to gaze at the ghost image of the owl-like floodlit Temple-Church aloft. It seemed balanced on a mound of darkness, and the river coiled below, a snake.

The night was warm and clean. Scents of vacuumed rooms and automatically swept squares. And the antiseptic water.

Parked across the road was a large truck, permitted the pavement, as it was in the process of delivery. Some other club or restaurant, for which vast blocks of treated ice were being brought, imbued with flowers.

Leocadia became aware of a noise behind her. It had been cloaked until now in the humming murmurs and squeals of the City.

She looked back.

Leocadia widened her eyes in contemptuous astonishment.

Pir had followed her through the narrow byways, and Jacqueline the obese nymph, and a tirade of others, all squashed and teetering in their polished or satin shoes, tight pants, and fishtail skirts. They bore their glasses of antacid champagne and laughed and called to her.

"Come back, my Leocadia!" howled Pir.

The two men unloading the truck stared at Leocadia. Between them they tilted a block of ice filled with a glowing fan of marigolds.

Leocadia came to the men and hauled the ice, burning, *burning*, from their gloved hands.

"Pardon me."

She flung the heavy chunk across the exit from the thin street, into the shoes and ankles of the approaching herd.

The ice shattered and smoked, and white sparks burst up from the chemicals of the ice treatment, causing Leocadia's pursuers to leap backward, some squawking and falling down.

The delivery men did not protest, they guffawed.

Leocadia saw marigolds, frozen flawless, the flowers of the eternal deathless soul, glittering in heaps and shoals like flamy fish, and splinters of ice, one of which had torn the fat knee of Jacqueline Dagot so she roared.

And then Leocadia lifted her skirt in her hand and she ran. For the bridge, the upper bank, over the river, into the night, toward the house and her sanctuary. Not knowing why, and not even particularly stung or startled. Instinct. Hunted. But so far, arrogant.

As she entered her street close by the Roman wall, Leocadia saw the darkness of the houses under the flare of the lamps that never failed. Rituals of decorum had come back to the City, and its fashionable quarters rose and bedded early. The manners of a century before, as with clothing, furnishing, but not always thought.

Yet on the street of dark houses, one light burned. It was in the attic room that Leocadia had made her studio.

She did not think for a moment she had left it on. She had shut the studio door upon the finished painting (removed from the easel) at four—sixteen hours by the abandoned scale. Then the daylight had still been rich and full.

Was the light another challenge?

She walked up the steps and put her finger to the required panel. Recognizing her, her door let her in.

The hall was in blackness, and only her touch on the proper switch woke up the hall lamps.

She paused. There was nothing in the air to alert her, only perhaps a faint scent of ozone. And she recalled another tale of Paradis, where shells from the ocean had been found at the doors of the Temple-Church, some manifestation of the primeval days when the City had been covered still by a hot and saline sea—or else a practical joke.

Leocadia climbed the stairs softly. Her hands were empty but flexed.

On the third landing she sought the smaller, crooked stair that went to the attic.

There was a faint electricity there, as if something had passed swiftly, voltage rather than presence.

Leocadia turned a fashionable enamel doorknob.

Her studio opened before her, a cave covered now by a black glass roof without even the moon. But the work lights shone down pitilessly, casting out shadow.

Leocadia's eyes went intuitively to her easel, a big bulky frame of metal that would support her largest canvases.

There was a new canvas there.

It hung by the crooks of its elbows, a sort of parody of a crucifixion. The head was thrown back and the neck arched. The breasts jutted erotically, but . . .

The nipples of the breasts were a blaring raw orange, and between the hapless female knees, emanating from the secret zone of sex and life, a curl of orange bled with a menstrual suddenness.

There were orange patterns, too, on the white flesh. Abstractions, looking like a map of unknown islands.

Leocadia experienced the sharp sour champagne, partially digested, creeping back into her mouth. She swallowed it, and walked around the canvas to its back.

There, tilted over, was the head and hair of Asra, known as Leocadia had known the naked form.

Something horrible had happened with Asra's head. Its eyes bulged and showed white. Between the lips was wedged a tube of brilliant orange paint, it had been squeezed to poison and to choke. Orange dribbled from the nostrils and the ears out into the silky fleece of hair.

Leocadia bent double and fire burst from her belly.

Far away, as this happened, she heard a tremendous crash, the roots of the house exploding.

As she stood up, wiping her mouth, and fell again and got up again, holding to the wall, a renewal of the sound of pursuit—the herd—drove up to the house, snorting and thundering on all the stairs.

The attic door bounced open.

It was like a party trick. For there they all were. Pir and Jacqueline and Claude Ful, and behind them Nanice and the peculiar Monsieur Saume. And then four men in white, who moved forward into the room.

Jacqueline began to shriek, as if she had been paid to do so.

Leocadia ignored her. The men in the white coats came right up to Leocadia.

"Now, now," said one fawningly.

"Poor Asra, it's what she feared," said Claude.

And Nanice exclaimed, "I warned you all—she's mad."

They had broken in the door below, and somewhere was the note of a police siren, rushing to contend with the door alarm.

"Oh, no police," said Nanice. "Our family name—"

Leocadia discerned a stinging in her arm, like the pincers of an angry beetle. She looked and saw the needle drawing away. The room wheeled and flew up into the dark.

After Van Orles and Saume had gone, sunset bloomed on the walls of Leocadia's room, deepening the colors of the broken ship that spilled glass and fruit.

On impulse Leocadia had painted a few shells into one corner of the picture, an insulting gesture, as if to overinform the watcher that this was the *sea*.

The room of pale gray was very plain, the furniture comfortable but modern, therefore unsumptuous, a large couch, small tables, a bed with a fearful plastic underlay. In the bathroom the fixtures were white and functional, and the floor was laid with stark black and white tiles, which leapt like rats at her blurred morning eyes.

Leocadia went to the door of the room, which opened. Past eight o'clock, or whenever presumably darkness came, the door did not open.

In the corridor was a hygienic nothingness.

Leocadia stepped to the elevator, which bore her seamlessly down to the garden.

The garden was a long slope of lawn, the grass seared by summer. A birdbath without water mocked the sky. At the bottom of the lawn stood a summerhouse, with curious windows of the shades of cinnamon and milk. Beyond, trees marked a boundary. A gravel walk led away, toward the crumbling biscuit buildings of the old asylum, as unlike the Residence as was possible. Black windows stared from those tall blocks, and copper pipes protruded from the shortbread walls. Between these monoliths and the modern site, an ancient hothouse, broken, held the corpse of an enormous grapevine, the black and withered grapes mummified upon it.

Huge outer barricades secured the entire complex. Within the labyrinth, you might wander as you wished, unable, ultimately, to get out.

Leocadia walked down to the summerhouse in the brazen glow. On a bench sat Mademoiselle Varc, a madwoman, who always mistook Leocadia for someone from her past.

"Have you brought my fan?" demanded Mademoiselle Varc.

"I'm sorry. It's been mislaid."

"Tssk," said Mademoiselle Varc. She had wispy white hair piled unsuccessfully upon her head, a white shawl. She was a White Queen, and twice as crazy.

"There goes the sun," said Leocadia.

"Goodbye!" cried Mademoiselle Varc, waving.

The sun eased behind the walls of the modern block.

"You're late," said Mademoiselle Varc.

"I'm sorry."

"Soon the police will be here."

As dusk came, wardens stole through the garden, shepherding inmates back to their rooms. Everyone went quietly, for they were always fairly demure. No need for needles, or truncheons.

"The police—yes."

"I miss the sunset," said Mademoiselle Varc. "It used to be so lovely. But now it takes only a moment or two, as in India, you know."

The sun vanished. A bat flew over the compound, exquisite wild thing, ignorant of barriers.

Then a uniformed man came walking up the gravel way. He raised his hand to the two women.

"Time to go in, ladies."

"You know what it is," said Mademoiselle Varc, taking Leocadia's arm and hurrying her back up the lawn.

"No."

"It's that the trees come alive after dark. They stump about the garden and catch anyone who's abroad. They tear them limb from limb, and eat them."

"How terrible," said Leocadia.

"Yes, it is."

She had woken in that bed, that sanitary bed with the plastic underlay, which creaked as she moved, making her think for a moment she lay in a hammock. The room rocked, certainly, but this was the aftereffect of the drug they had injected into her. And as she remembered that, she remembered it all.

A couple of minutes later the door opened, and a friendly dark-clad young woman entered with a tray of breakfast. Rolls and conserves, fruit, coffee, and a little pot of tea.

"I take vodka with my breakfast," said Leocadia, from the bed.

"I'll fetch you some from your refrigerator, mademoiselle."

And sure enough, she went into an alcove and returned with a bottle and a tall glass. "It's nice and cold, mademoiselle. The way you like it. Anything you want can be ordered and kept there. And there's a heater, besides, for making hot drinks."

"This isn't a hotel," said Leocadia. The girl smiled nicely.

Leocadia got out of bed, and the room gradually righted itself. There was the bathroom, black and white and clean as disinfectant.

When she emerged, the attendant was gone.

As she ate a roll and drank her vodka, Leocadia explored the confine. She did not try the door, which she assumed would be locked. (It was not.)

On one wall was a shelf of books, which in turn, at the press of a switch, gave on an alcove also lined with books. These were her own, it seemed, or most of them. She saw at once there were new titles, volumes on art and design, current novels, treatises on animal and human behavior.

At the other end of the room, beyond the bed and the sitting area, was a broad space. An easel leaned against the wall, and three canvases, unprepared, beside it. Leocadia's worktable stood by, loaded with paints and accessory impedimenta. The light was excellent, windows on both sides of the room, and a light source above the painting space, nearly as good as the attic.

Leocadia went to both the windows.

The one beyond the bed looked out across the slope of garden to the summerhouse. Behind that were the trees, and then the vague shapes in sunshine of colossal block buildings, utterly square in form, indefinably blind, like a deserted factory—or a prison.

The window at the other end of the room showed only a high wall, but it was grown with blackish ivies, not unpleasant.

She tried the windows. Each gave easily, admitting light and air and the song of crickets and birds.

The distance to the ground was three stories. Too far to jump.

She knew at once that Nanice had had her restricted in some institution, but she was not aware exactly of what kind.

She considered dead Asra. Could Leocadia even be sure that she had seen such a thing? Was it some obscene jest, or the result of some tablet slipped into the poor champagne?

No. It must be real. What other excuse for her confinement here?

She thought of the dead Asra with a combination of revulsion and rage.

Leocadia was supposed to have killed Asra.

But what had happened, in fact? Who had done it?

Asra had been able to enter the house as she wished, since Leocadia had not blanked out her recognition on the door. But thereafter Asra must have let in whoever it was that attacked her. Was it some other lover, or only some maniac?

The police had obviously been fobbed, or bought off. There would have been enough money for that.

Perhaps because of the drug that had been given her, or other more insidious medicines administered in food sleep, through the medium of light and sound, Leocadia did not at this point decipher that Asra had been specifically murdered in order to cast blame upon Leocadia.

Presently, an envelope of plastic paper came through a slit in the door. She impatiently opened it.

A small printed slip fell into her hand. Someone hoped she had spent a restful night and enjoyed her breakfast. The music panel beside her bed, which would bring her whatever music she selected, would also inform her of the time. At fourteen, some of her doctors would be coming to see her.

This friendly note was not signed.

Leocadia dialed the time on the panel. Thirteen—one o'clock.

In a closet off the bathroom she found some of her own clothes—a selection, but nothing dressy for the evening or dinner.

When she was dressed, had brushed her hair, and had used her makeup—located in a drawer of the dressing table near the window—Leocadia sat on the couch to wait.

Probably, they were punctual.

There were four of them.

They wore smart urbane suits, nothing clinical, and Dr. Van Orles sported a pastal cravat, Dr. Leibiche had a monocle. Dr. Duval wore his hair rather long, with a mustache. Dr. Saume, unfortunately for him, was as she remembered.

They were all ugly, squat men, not obese but having the look of partially inflated balloons. As they dressed in the fashionable pre-century style, just so they had kept old-fashioned unsightlinesses, of teeth in the case of Saume, warts and pimples in the case of Leibiche.

They sat in a semicircle on the three low chairs, with Dr. Duval draped on the other end of the couch.

Then, in a dreadfully personal, insolent gesture, Saume leaned forward and felt Leocadia's pulse.

She allowed this, but when he leaned nearer with some sort of glass to stare into her eyes, she pushed him back.

"Now mademoiselle, we only want to see how you are."

"Angry," said Leocadia. "What else would you expect?"

Perhaps they had expected fright?

"Oh, but there's nothing to be concerned at," said Duval, his hair sliding and slipping about like spilled unguent. "Indeed, you *shouldn't* concern yourself. You must try to be as quiet as you can."

"I was drugged and abducted. Why should I be quiet?"

Saume cleared his throat. He announced, with the gentle gravity of a father who must be stern with a child for its own sake: "Mademoiselle, a fearful thing has been done. A murder has been committed." And then, a phenomenon occurred, a hellish glare seemed to spring up around Saume, a sort of spotlight. A sign of impending ills .... "You must understand," he snarled, "only the intervention of your cousins has permitted your enclosure here, at the Residence. Otherwise it would have been the *jail.* Your sentence would have been severe. But under the circumstances, and with the proper evidence we have been able to gather on your critical state of mind, we are able to shelter you here. And here, of course, we may hope to cure you. One day, you may go free."

Leocadia had conquered fear in childhood. But it is a fact with fear that it tends to return in other guises and must be fought off again and again. Eventually, through dint of effort, it may find some means to throw you down into the abyss.

She clenched her hands, but then undid them, seeing all the beady eyes, and the extra eye of the monocle, glinting on her.

They had told her they were doctors, and that she was "sheltered" in the Residence. She had dimly heard of it. A building that rose above Paradis, in the hills, safely out of the environs of the City. The lunatic asylum.

The glare still shone about them. Was it some trick of the sun, or some trick of theirs? Or a warning from her own mind?

She was in the Madhouse, but now it was not even a hospital, but a professed *House*.

She said, "So I killed Asra?"

"You will have blanked the act from your brain, mademoiselle," said Leibiche. "This is common."

"It may be a hopeful sign," added Van Orles. "Indicating that you feel remorse for the deed."

Leocadia, used to saying what she thought, stayed herself. "You said I killed Asra. How did I do it, when I was with so many people at the Surprise?"

The glare fastened on Van Orles and blazed.

"But it was before you left for the restaurant, Leocadia."

"Oh, I see. How sensible."

Leocadia beheld then all the counters of the game lying before her, but it would be a while longer before she set them into their true positions. Before she drew the obvious conclusion.

Hungry for all the spoils of Uncle Michelot's death, Nanice and the cousins, perhaps even those two reckoned to have been made up, had had to prove Leocadia incapable of inheriting. And Asra—stupid, petty, pretty, *living* Asra—had died for their convenience, the stepping stone to topple Leocadia down. They had killed her, had her killed. Orange paint, and cold blood.

Confronted by the four doctors, Leocadia saw at last that she was sunk into deep water. The light glare faded.

She glanced at the easel, the waiting canvases, and said with a deadly compunction, "What am I supposed to do here?"

"Everything you wish, mademoiselle. Don't imagine there are any harsh measures. The old techniques were often crude, but they are long gone." Saume nodded.

"We shall," said Duval kindly, "simply take care of you."

"Talk to you," added Van Orles, "observe your progress."

"You've lived a life that has placed upon you," said Leibiche, "terrible unconscious strains. Once these are eliminated, we shall make headway." His monocle and all his warts and spots flashed like sequins in a smile.

"How dangerous am I reckoned to be?" asked Leocadia. "Since you think me a murderess."

"Ah!" Saume blinked as if startled. Why? "Come now," he said firmly. "With correct supervision, you'll grow calm."

"Things in the food," said Leocadia.

"The most harmless, naturally produced and nourishing—"

"But I'm given a knife for my butter," said Leocadia, "and over there is my palette knife. Also my nail file."

"We trust you," said Doctor Duval.

It flashed upon her, like the fireworks of the warts, that perhaps she was to be left potential weapons in order that she turn them on herself. For this she did know at once, she would never be free.

There would be no "cure." Since she was not ill, not mad, not a murderess, or anything else they said.

All they would want to do, rather than make her better, was to change her into the Leocadia of their invention. Nanice's Leocadia, who killed and was insane.

TWO

Paradys

A trick that everyone abhors
In little girls is slamming doors.

Belloc

Hilde.

Although they had just put her into corsets and long
frocks, she was fifteen, and still a child. Pale and perfect.
Skin milk white, hair a shining wonderful ginger, now piled
up upon her head with tortoiseshell combs.

She did what little girls were meant to do. She was obedient and loving but not importunate. She had a doll who sat
on her bed of frills and flounces. She read fine books of
which her mother was the guardian. Her father, Monsieur
Koster, was a wealthy man, descendant of a merchant family.
Now high enough in society, he took care to comport himself
with great dignity. Sometimes he chose also a book for Little
Hilde to read (she was to them "Little Hilde"). She embroi-
dered too. Her mother had begun to train her in the rituals of
wifeship, seeing that the house of polished stairs, lace curtains, and huge ferns in china bowls ran on butter.

And Hilde was happy. It was a safe existence where
everything was in its place. God ruled the world. Her father
ruled the house. Her mother ruled her. But all three were
kind and might be pleaded with prettily for favors. Which
they would then grant. God was especially amenable: "Let
me not have freckles, like Angeline," and God did not allow
Hilde to become freckled. (Her father did not care for

39

freckles.) And her mother would let Hilde buy sweets once a week. Her father permitted Hilde to try a sip of wine at dinner. "It's good for the child's blood."

But Hilde had a secret life. It did not occur to her to share it, let alone confess. It had to do with darkness and her narrow bed, the touch of the linen nightgown on her bareness, and of her hair in a long plait that she might undo, always to the consternation of her maid in the morning: "However did this happen?" And Hilde would be innocent and surprised. For in her heart she knew that her undone hair was not a crime, nor what sometimes happened to her in the dark. They were silly childish things, very pleasant, like playing with the doll, or eating a sweet. Somehow, not so public. A game of childhood out of which, of course, as a woman she would grow, ascending into a cold clever angel, the peerless wife, and adorable admirable mother, in her turn, of other little children.

But the dark . . . The dark was lovely. A special thing she could do. A sort of present. She doubted anyone else in the world was able to.

And strangely, sometimes when she did this marvelous thing, which left her whole body ringing and tingling, beautifully composed for sleep, she had an incoherent image of some weight that pinned her to the bed, and that the hands upon her were not her own. And now and then, she would kiss the pillow, but not as she kissed her mother or papa. She wished the pillow then was more like a fruit, sweeter, and more moist. Once she had dreamed that it was, and in slumber the lovely thing happened on its own. She was amazed and gratified. Truly, it was a gift, and she was sorry she would have to grow out of it.

She had feared slightly, when the corset had been compressed about her and the long dress put on and her hair raised up, that this might be the end of her game.

But it was not. Oddly, in some curious way, it actually heightened her enjoyment. How lucky. How sad for Mama and Papa that they had never known such a thing and never, now, would.

The Koster house was one of a group of elegant mansions high on Clock Tower Hill. Smart carriages drawn by satin horses speeded up and down the street, and trees overhung the pavement. In the mornings, maids might be seen scrubbing the steps, and gardeners toiled over the flowers against the railings.

Two months after the putting up of Hilde's ginger cloud of hair, Madame Koster descended the steps of the house with her daughter. Their carriage stood ready on the street with a man holding open the door. The lady and her child were going to see a play at the Goddess of Tragedy. It was an epic from an era before the Revolution, poetic prose, three hours of it. A stern moral tale, incidentally full of drama, passion, bloodshed, and terror. The afternoon performance had therefore been thought most suitable.

Everyone in Paradys who might be said to be anybody was to attend at some point. Wishing to go, Madame Koster had assured monsieur the play was a classic, and should be part of Hilde's education.

Hilde, as a girl, had been tutored at home, and these classical plays were sometimes gone through by a pie-faced governess with a high squeaky voice. Something of their power was therefore lost on Hilde, who accordingly did not look forward to the jaunt, save that it was the theater. For this, since her earliest pantomimes, she had cherished a beglamored enthusiasm. She was too, so far, a patient girl. She had been trained to be. It had also occurred to her that while the play went on, if it was very boring, there would be the audience to scan (surreptitiously in the gloom) and thoughts of other things to be gone over—her doll's new wardrobe, a patch of garden behind the house that was hers, and so on.

The Goddess of Tragedy towered white and tiered above the streets. Many mothers and daughters, and some young sons, were assembled. "Why," said Madame Benoit to Madame Koster, "have you not heard of the actor who is playing the Roman?"

"No not at all."

"Well, he is quite astonishing. He has brought the part to life. They say it's frightful, his moment of death."

Soon Hilde was installed in the plush Koster box. Her mother had not agreed to bonbons or chocolates. It was not that sort of play.

Hilde sat quietly, and having viewed the fashionable afternoon gowns, she saw the gas lamps lowered, and the heavy curtain rose.

For twenty minutes it was very dull. So dull that even obedient Hilde felt a faint jab of rebellion.

But then. Then, *he* came out. Out of the wings onto the plateau of the stage.

Stage light is always miraculous. It is a magical spell that breathes on things and changes them, *remakes* them. Besides, the creatures who people this universe have, very often, a psychic, extraordinary power. How else can they do what they do?

The man who characterized the Roman wore a costume of black and silver, the notion of the time as to what the garments of a Roman commander might have been. But he was tall and slender, with wide shoulders. He had a priest's face, and the arrogance of a priest, officiating at his altar. His hair was black as ravens. His eyes, blacker.

From the instant he emerged from nowhere onto the stage, Hilde understood, just as a bird grasps abruptly how to fly, that here was the reason for her instinct and her life. She did not have to question herself, or any other. She did not have the temerity to say to God: *Why?* Let alone, *No, no.*

Her body felt light as cobweb. Her heart was engorged and beat like a gong.

She floated somewhere just above the ledge of the box, and oddly, her mother could not see this. And Hilde knew quite well that the man below, so near, so far, the Roman, she knew that he must also be intensely aware of her. For she blazed like a lamp, and he, being what he was, must see all things exactly. He would sense her, and look up. And so he did. Up to the box, his eyes flaming like stars, over and over.

And then Hilde burned, and she must look away. But only, each time, for a moment.

The play, forgotten parts of which the squeaky governess may even have read to her, this time fixed itself into Hilde's mind. She was conscious of every iota of it, every histrionic, profound, and adult emotion. As if a door had been flung open before her, revealing a new world.

When it came time for the Roman to die, Hilde's gonging heart stopped. She felt herself die, too. And thereafter, what could she be save reborn?

She saw him again briefly, the actor-priest, taking his bows at the end of the play. He did this coldly and magnificently, as if to show them he had elevated the Host already, what more could they want? Only one further time did he raise his face toward Hilde's balcony. One ray (like a lighthouse). Then gone.

Hilde went home in the Koster carriage and in a dream, a trance. She had been ensorcelled.

"Hilde, eat your food."

"I'm sorry, Mama, I'm not hungry."

"What is the matter with the child. Are you unwell?"

"No, Mama."

They had not noticed how silent Little Hilde had become because she was generally a quiet, abstemious daughter, what they preferred.

"It's the weather," pronounced Monsieur Koster, "Eh, Hilde? Too hot. Take her for a drive, Lysette."

"We had a drive this morning, Solomon."

"Then probably the carriage was too stuffy."

"The carriage was perfect."

They lost interest in the carriage and Little Hilde, and Hilde was able to leave her unwanted luncheon for the maid to clear away.

As Hilde sat presently, her hands resting on an oval of unseen embroidery, she heard her mother speaking to a servant in the hall.

"We must have flowers there and there. And I shall want to see Cook. Some special light dishes that they can peck at like birds."

Hilde's mother was arranging an evening of guests, as she sometimes did. Madame Koster flowed back and forth and so into the sitting room, where she came to inspect Hilde's work. Hilde stitched at a rose.

"How listless you are," said Madame Koster. "Is it your time?" She was referring to Hilde's cycle of menstruation.

"No, Mama."

"I thought not. Well, you must liven up. You're becoming depressing. Tomorrow afternoon you must have a fitting for your new dress."

"Yes, Mama."

"What do you think?" said Madame Koster, a touch flustered all of a sudden. "Some of the theater people are coming to my little evening."

Hilde's hand stayed mute upon the rose.

"Well, you might show some interest, you tiresome girl. All lost in a world of your own. I don't think you need to meet my guests, but your father insists. You look so young and charming—why, you might only be eleven, except for your hair. . . . Perhaps we will have it dressed down for the night. It's so pretty that way."

Hilde's mother always saw Hilde as very young, and Hilde did not ever question this, nor why it was an extra delight to her mother if Hilde should remain very young. At this minute, in any case, she was not thinking of that.

"Who—will be coming to your party, Mama?"

"Oh, the two leading men of the company, Monsieur Roche and Monsieur Martin. And a couple of the ladies, I believe. But of course you've forgotten all about that important play. What a disappointment you were. Everyone else bubbling over and not a word out of you. I half think you slept right through it."

"Oh no, Mama."

"Well, then, who are Monseur Roche and Monsieur Johanos Martin?" demanded Mama, bridling. She was flushed,

44

but exclaimed, "And well you should blush, Hilde, You've quite forgotten."

Hilde lowered her burning face.

"Monsieur Johanos Martin played the Roman."

"One out of two then," snapped Madame Koster.

She was a tallish woman, curvaceous, with fashionable apparent mounds of hair built up over padding on her skull. Her maid knew many of her secrets. The coiffeur, the rouge, the manner in which madame sometimes lost her temper as the corset refused to reduce her waist below twenty-four inches. Hilde's waist, uncorseted, was eighteen inches, and in its cage of bones became a flower stalk. Her hair grew in lush masses, her skin was fresh as if the dew were on it.

Sometimes the maid privately wondered if madame allowed Hilde so many sweets in hopes of extra girth, or blotches. Hilde had not wanted sweets this week.

"Your new frock is very lovely and young," said madame. "You'll grow up too fast. And you're such a baby."

In the dark . . .

Hilde woke. She had been dreaming.

In the dream, the party had begun, and through the crowd of guests Hilde had found herself moving, not dressed as she should be, but in her long white nightgown, and her hair loose on her shoulders. No one had appeared to notice, and after her first terrifying shame, she began to think that perhaps she was dressed quite properly.

Then, by the open door that led onto the little terrace, he was standing. He wore black clothes, she could not make them out, not his costume from the play, certainly, yet neither anything everyday. A sort of soutane, perhaps, a priestly robe, belted close at the thin hard waist.

He had looked straight at her, Johanos Martin, the actor. And, impossibly, she had met his gaze, although her ears roared and her heart choked her.

Everyone else was gone. It did not matter how or where. He held out his hand, which was ringless, beautiful, and

Hilde went to him at once. He drew her out of the door onto the terrace.

Night had fallen, very black, yet with a sort of silver glow along the tops of the trees, and far away a light was shining that might have been the moon reflected on a window— such detail, in this dream.

"You are mine," Johanos Martin said to Hilde. "I promise I will be with you."

And in that exquisite second, she woke. She woke.

She lay stunned, not knowing, or caring, where she was, out of situation and time. And her body was alive, glowing and spangled by feeling within and without.

She had not, since she had seen him, somehow—she had not dared to touch. But now her hands stole to her body. She laid them on her breasts. And in the dark, eyes shut, she thought of his hands lying on her in this way, firm and cruel, capturing her breasts like birds. And then she thought that she would be afraid, half fainting, and he would hold her up, easily, and crush her mouth with his, as in a book she had once seen, a book of her mother's that perhaps she had not been meant to find, the drawing of a man kissing a woman fiercely in this way, holding her swooning and bent back as if he preyed on her.

Hilde trembled violently. Her stomach churned and sank and melted. Her fingers ran lightly down and touched her there, at last, in the secret place.

"I am yours," she whispered to Johanos Martin, as he bent her back, supporting her, his mouth on hers. And shivers of fire ran upward through her body, familiar and yet unique. Her loins seemed to rock at the impact of deep, rare blows. And the door that had opened in her brain flew open in her womb, showering her with suns and comets, shaking her end to end. She cried out before she could prevent it.

Two minutes later her maid came in with a lamp.

"What is it, Mademoiselle Hilde? You do look hot."

"A dream," muttered Hilde. The first time she had had to practice true deception.

"There, there. Well I must get on if you're better."

"Quite better, thank you."

The maid removed herself. Hilde wept. She did not know why. But she was racked again by tears silenced in the pillow that once, misunderstanding, she had kissed.

The magic art of the night sprang from him, then. He had sent it ahead of him. He too had always known. He and she.

Her innocence was gone, not her naïveté.

She scarcely slept again that night. The doll lay on the floor.

Madame Koster stood in her upstairs sitting room, turning about to regard her dress of ivory satin. From beyond her windows and their cumbersome drapes, the ripe westering light of the late summer evening flattered her with its glow.

A knock, and Little Hilde's maid entered.

"What is the matter with her?"

"She's been sick again, madame."

"Really. Such a stupid child. Well, I can't attend a sickroom now. She must be put to bed."

"Monsieur gave orders that Mademoiselle Hilde be given a glass of white wine."

"Did he indeed? How will that help? It will make her stomache worse."

"No, madame. He said it was very cooling, for the stomache, and that her vomiting was all nerves, so the wine will do her good."

"Nerves! What nerves? I am the one with nerves. She's just a child."

Along the passage in her room, Hilde sat pale as death on a sofa, staring at the glass of wine on the tray as if it were poison.

"Take a sip. It can't hurt."

The maid too was irritated. Madame took it out on her when the daughter did not turn out right.

"But I feel—"Hilde broke off, swallowing rapidly, like a cat before it pukes.

"Well, madame wants me downstairs, so I must go."

Hilde was only relieved to be left alone.

This was the hour of her most awful trial. She had longed for and dreaded this festivity of her mother's, not realizing her emotion would build to such a pitch that she would be made sick by it.

Suddenly she got up, and seizing the wineglass, she put it to her mouth. Like a despairing damsel in a play, she dashed the potion through her lips and swallowed all of it. Then she stood amazed.

Almost instantly her sickness swelled to an orchestral tumult—and perished. It was gone, leaving her light and slightly afloat. A pulse beat in her temples. Hilde laughed. This too was part of the magic. Her dear wise papa had helped her to safety. She had been lifted above the demons and made whole. For him, the one who would soon be with her.

In her turn, freed now, Hilde moved about to regard herself, her clothes and her hair.

Her mother had aimed for a veneer of complete childishness, but the dressmaker had maliciously somehow done something to the frock, so that it was merely very simple, very fresh. And the effect of the loose, slightly coiling amber hair gave, rather than the impression of a little girl, the look of one of the mysterious beauties of current paintings, maidens from legend, standing in bowers, as knights rode by.

Hilde was happy at herself, guessing this, not understanding. Happy to be lovely, not realizing that she was.

He would recognize her. As she had recognized him.

Half an hour later, she descended to the salon.

The event had already begun, and Madame Koster was at its hub. She looked at Hilde askance a moment, as if not knowing who she was. Perhaps sensible: Does one ever know another, or who they are, let alone a "child"?

But monsieur had not yet come in. He was, in fact, rather at odds with the party. It meant he must dress up very stiffly and parade his grandeur to impress them all, and this was onerous on such a hot evening.

There were many people in the salon. They drank from glasses of champagne. And since the servant came also to Hilde—again, was it some sort of conspiracy?—and offered her the drink, Hilde took it wonderingly, and sipped.

Then the crowd parted, and she saw the window that led out to the garden. No one was there. *He* was not.

Hilde sighed, and a fearful intimation of darkness crossed her, like the shadow of a huge, transparent crow.

Would he not come? Why should he come? Never before had actors been invited to these show gatherings. Why had her mother done it?

Oh, but it was all part of the starry plan, of destiny. It must be.

Three women approached Hilde. They were ladies she had met before, acquaintances of her mother's. Her heart slid down as if to hide itself.

"Why look, who's this? Is it Little Hilde? A young lady at last."

"What a becoming dress. How clever of your mother. And the hair's an exact copy of *Ygraine Waiting for Uther.*"

"Do you have it brushed every night? One hundred strokes are essential."

A wing lifted off the room. Everything shifted slightly, an earth tremor.

Hilde's mother skated across the chamber. She met in the door the two tall actors from the Goddess of Tragedy. They were unmistakable. And all at once the crowd broke into applause.

Hilde thought: *For him.*

Fanfares of trumpets and showers of petals.

She drank all the champagne in her glass, the magic potion that, rather than make her invisible, would allow her to be seen.

She watched Monsieur Martin enter the salon.

Her mother deferred to him even more than to Monsieur Roche, who, walking behind, looked down the slope of his long face. No, it was Monsieur Martin that Madame Koster drew into the very core of her house, and kept there, so the wine could be rushed to him and the guests flutter up like greedy moths.

How cold he looked. Cruel, but one would not call it cruel, not if one wished for his kindness. Cold and cruel and closed and *set*.

Seen in life away from the stage, his face was pale, and the eyes were not black but a glacial gray. Nor was he handsome, yet there was that in his face which magnetized, some affirmation.

He did glance about him, but saw no one. Then he spoke graciously, and even smiled a little at the ones who clustered around him. He drank the champagne, several glasses of it.

Hilde remained at the edge of the congregation, like the shell in a story, left behind by the ghost of a primordial sea at the foot of the Temple-Church.

He would see her now, or now. And she waited for this finding gaze, this instant of pure acknowledgment, stretched taut as the string of a lyre. But it did not come.

And gradually something gave way a little at the center of her physical and etheric frame. Only a tiny derangement. It should have warned her. But how should she know it?

Presently they went into the supper room. Madame Koster sat at one end of the dainty table, and the actors sat either side of her, Monsieur Martin to her right. Monsieur Koster, who had blustered in after all, too late to be properly noticed, thumped down at the table's opposite end, and in the upheaval, no place had been allotted Hilde. So she sat among some of the men and women who knew her, in the bars of the trap of their patronage.

She could not eat a thing, but she sipped the wine. Some of the ladies noticed and disapproved. "That girl is taking too much. What is her mother thinking of?" "Of Johanos Martin," whispered another lady behind her fan.

Hilde did not hear this. She watched the lord who had given his promise to her in a dream, but carefully. It was not subtlety or care that made her careful. Rather she sensed the fire of herself, so bright, so piercing. She dared not be obvious.

He never looked her way.

Never.

After the supper, Monsieur Roche, a little tipsy, agreed to give a speech from the play. This was second best, but of course Johanos Martin would not perform. He had modestly and arrogantly refused.

Monsieur Roche, though the worse for wine, was very good.

The night had dropped like velvet on the garden. The lamps were lit along the paths, and up against the two small statues Monsieur Koster had had imported.

The guests walked in the soft air.

Madame Koster was arm in arm with Monsieur Martin. However had she achieved it? He looked disdainful, faintly amused. She seemed to take this for his interest.

Monsieur Koster was arguing about business in the salon with three gentlemen from a famous bank.

Hilde walked out between the hedges.

It had taken all her nerve, all the six glasses of wine she had consumed.

Unlike Monsieur Roche, Hilde Koster was not drunk. She was a maenad, given over to the god, and balanced in his hand. But had she mistaken the wrong god for the real one? For the real god of the wine is the god of self-knowing, dark twin of Apollo, black sun of opening and rebirth. Dionysos offers often painful truth with the wine, but he does not actually *lie*. Hilde's god, maybe, was all a lie, and that was what the look of affirmation was, a wonderful, successful sham. Like acting itself.

"Oh—" exclaimed Madame Koster. She was caught in the state known among mothers and daughters. Here was the fruit of her body, which she had loved, and perhaps still did love. Only not now a joy, but an interruption. Worse, a reminder.

And Johanos Martin looked from his height. And noticed Hilde.

She was very beautiful. Better than the poor little mutilated classical statues. Better by far than the women of the house. He did not want her, for he had already what he wanted. But still, he looked. At last, he saw.

"My daughter," said madame. "My little girl. Hilde. This is the great actor Johanos Martin."

Hilde gazed up, for a while half blinded by his eyes. Then she glanced down. She held out her hand because she had long ago been taught to do so. All sense had left her, it was automatic.

"Mademoiselle," said Johanos Martin. And he bowed. That was all.

"Come," said Hilde's mother, "your glass is empty, monsieur." And she led him back toward the terrace by the window, where the servant had appeared with long glinting goblets.

"I'm afraid, madame, I must take my leave," said Monsieur Martin.

"But no—such a lovely night—this garden air is so good for you after—"

"Ah, madame, you must permit me to know what is good for me."

Madame Koster was speechless. Unfortunately, she had got used to people who rarely said what they meant.

And so he slipped from her clutches like the sea.

The two women, one middle-aged and sour, one young and blighted, stood on the walk and watched the cold priest stride away, back to his church of Tragedy.

In her room, Hilde became hysterical.

Naturally, she had not meant to. It was a reaction to the wine, and to grief. (Was Ophelia only drunk?)

She wept in the way one screams.

The maid ran for tired, soured madame.

And madame came like a storm.

"What is the matter with you? Ridiculous noisy child! Be *quiet!* Here I am with a migraine and all this racket."

Hilde tried to stay her tears, her shrieking sobs, for she was accustomed to obey.

But the grief was new. It ravaged her. She was torn. How,

with her entrails ripped from her body, could she be calm and quiet?

"Well—what is it?"

"Oh, Mama—"

But Hilde did not say what it was. There is a knowledge beyond knowing. Besides, how to speak of the unspeakable? Persuaded to the throne of love, and pushed aside.

"Hurry—three drops of my mixture, quick. Give it her; for God's sake."

The drops were administered. On top of the wine they worked wonders. Hilde was violently sick again, and eventually, exhausted by these humiliations, tumbled into sleep.

Is death this? To wake in a vault and swim slowly upward, and there to meet the blows of memory?

O God— O God— But God had gone deaf.

In her virgin's bed, Hilde wept. Softly now, as after the ecstasy in the dark. Must not be heard. No one must find her. For who would help?

Her maid chided her for not arising. Then for not touching the invalid breakfast.

Madame came, and chided too.

Hilde lay like a wounded snake, spineless, broken.

Then she heard a woman, some gypsy, singing in the street. Servants from the houses chased her off. And Hilde wept again.

But then she thought, *He bowed to me.*

And she recalled how his eyes had, finally, seen her.

But her mother had been by. And all the people. And the lights.

Perhaps . . .

Hilde got up and went to her mirror. She was so young, even after the outburst of anguish and tears, still she was what she had been. And somehow her youth infallibly told her she was not yet destroyed.

Of course, there were concerns surrounding him. In the story, the knight must win the notice of the lady. And she, Hilde, she must win his notice.

What could she take to him? Only herself. Surely he must see. Surely, surely, he must know.

She would die for him. That was enough. She must be brave. She must seek him out. Alone. Alone he could not fail to find her, as she, amid a crowd of hundreds, had found him.

Hilde washed and dressed and put up her hair and went down.

Monsieur Koster was at home, and beholding her, he beamed. He had heard she had been naughty, but now she was only his pretty, nice little daughter, his very own, that one day he would sell for a high profit in the marriage market Babylon of Paradys.

"Well, Hilde, got over your sulks?"

"Yes, Papa. I'm sorry, Papa."

"You mustn't be a bad girl. You worry your mother and then she worries your poor papa. A young lady must be demure and gentle. Loving and giving. Docile. Not these unbecoming tantrums and noise."

Hilde drifted past a mirror, and some radiant, true, but deceiving part of her called in her soul: *No one can ignore this. This youth and bloom, this being and nature.*

Loving and giving.

THREE

Paradise

▲

Who put the "art" in heart, the "pain" in paint,
and the ice in Pardise?

John Kaiine

Smara walked through the night mist of the City, under her floating lamp. One hand she kept against the rough and stony, dripping surfaces of walls. In the other, she carried a long and slender knife. This was her left hand. She was naturally right-handed but had trained herself to left-handedness. It had been her first curtsy to the craziness of her world.

She was on the path beside a canal. A snake, perhaps, glicked and eddied through the water, but she could not see it, only the blurred ripples picked up by the lamp.

Then, footsteps.

Smara waited, and a man came from the mist. He wore graceful gray garments, and a mask like a black bird.

"Beloved—how extraordinary to meet you here," he exclaimed. And held out his arms to Smara.

She went to him, and plunged the knife slantwise into his throat. Blood sprayed like thick drops of jet, some hitting the lamp in the air, but it quickly shook them off.

The man soon fell dead on the towpath, and Smara bent over him. She removed from his finger a ring of twisted bronze, and then dragged the bird mask from his face. Beneath he too had the face of a bird, beaked nose, tiny mouth, protuberant sideways eyes. Smara held her breath in dismay.

She stood up and hurried away, having only paused to wipe her knife on the bird man's sleeve.

The third bridge had long ago collapsed into the river. It was feasible to go halfway across it, and then to jump into the mercury-colored water and swim for shore. To those who sat in the bar above the strand, the intermittent splashes of these jumps were broadcast spasmodically.

A woman danced naked on a table to the tune of a comb.

Felion sat drinking from a jug of water drawn out of the river. It was highly toxic, more inebriating than any liquor.

Smara went to him and gave him the ring. There was a trace of blood on it. He put it on, and handed her four brushes of wonderful springing hair.

"He was painting shells on the ground in the porch of the church. A shame it was a painter I killed. He was quite talented. But the shells will stay. He didn't smudge them as he convulsed all over the stone."

"Mine wore a bird mask," said Smara.

She drank some water and closed her eyes. She was very pale.

A man came by with a tray of lizard-scaled, fanged fish snared from the river. Felion bought one, and put it into his drink. It revived and swam about. He threw it from an open smashed window, back into the river.

"What are we to do?" said Smara. "Oh, what?"

"Let's go into our uncle's labyrinth."

"No," she said. "No."

"Let me remind you of his will. He had accrued property and funds in the other city—the *sane* city. These riches would come to us. We could live there."

"But to walk through the ice . . ."

"Don't be afraid," he said. His face was beautiful with compassion. "Smara, what can hurt us worse than *here*?"

"I must kill again," she said abruptly.

"All right. Let's finish the jug, and then we'll go together."

Now she nodded. He refilled her glass twice, thrice.

A woman came by selling human eyes set into rings.

"How lovely," said Smara.

"They won't last," said the woman. "I'll sell you one for a kiss."

"Then kiss me."

The woman kissed her, briskly, and gave her one of the rings. The eye in it was pure, a crystal spherical gray.

"How much better than the ring I brought you."

Felion took her hand. "When we go out, you can throw it away."

She nodded. Two silver tears ran suddenly from her eyes. "I try so hard. It's as if I must. Do you remember Mother?"

"She's dead," he answered absently.

"I wish—"

"No, you don't wish that. Let's live. Come on, we'll kill."

They left the bar together and walked along the pebbly strand. From the banks of the City, gleams and glares spilled into the water. Someone leapt off the bridge and drowned.

"This way," he said. He led her up, onto the embankment, and then they turned into the upper City.

Out of the charcoal fog of nighttime Paradise, the open doorways gaped, shining. Here and there processions of citizens passed, chanting and banging gongs, or weeping, or utterly silent.

"Where are we going?" she said.

"To the Clock Tower Hill."

"Dogs run in the streets there," she said.

"Yes," he said, "and when we kill, it will feed them."

So they climbed up the heights of Paradise.

A bell was ringing in the cranium of the cathedral, but when they reached Clock Tower Hill, only the ticking of ancient apparatuses, mimicking clocks, was to be heard, and an occasional snarl.

Felion and Smara found people dancing around a bonfire and lured them off one by one, and sliced them to death in the shadows.

After about an hour of this, only two were left dancing by the fire. Felion and Smara joined them briefly, then stole away.

"Where now?"

"You know where, Smara."

"No, I won't."

"*Please.*"

They stood beneath a street lamp that still burned with a cold luminescence. Smara's personal lamp had faded.

"I won't enter the labryinth of our uncle."

"Then I must do it by myself."

Smara turned from him.

Lightless, she moved away like a ghost, down a slim alleyway under broken casements, into the fog.

As he climbed back up the hundred steps to his uncle's mansion, Felion experienced a partly irritated excitement.

When he gained the house, and it had let him in, he went at once to his uncle's study, or workroom, on the second floor. The room was built into a sort of tower and jutted out over the abyss of the steps. In the darkness, anything might have been below, a cliffside, even some sluggish silent sea.

Felion activated the mechanical lights, and then, sitting at the great black worktable, he reread portions of the rambling letter his uncle had left for him. (Smara, of course, had never consulted it.)

All about lay bizarre machines that did not now work, and which perhaps never had, and arrested experiments involving vials of glass and transparent plastic, coils of metal, balances, and fluids that had solidified. Over these the damp dust formed a second skin, in parts thick and vegetable as moss.

". . . I am a scientist who has always longed to be a poet," said the sonorous and self-indulgent letter. "Where, after all, is the difference? Scribbling down on scraps of paper equations and potential formulae, or snatches of mystical words, couplets that rhyme. My labyrinth is also a sonnet. It has its own meter, its own intrinsic meaning. One must reach the heart, and then the farther side, and so new knowledge. This requires concentration, but not necessarily courage. Nothing mechanistic can be taken into the maze.

No watch or other timepiece, no devices for measuring. Not even a gun, should you or your sister have come across such a weapon on your karma-collecting activities of murder. No mechanical lamp. You may use one of the torches I have prepared and left for you; each needs only a match to light it. As you pass through the ice of the labyrinth, the torch may melt it a little, but that is to the good. There will then always be a limit on the number of occasions you may go in and out. This isn't a game. You will have to decide whether you want your inheritance, a life in the second city beyond the maze."

Felion glanced about the study. One of the unreliable lamps fluttered, as if winking at him. He turned the page, and read:

"I myself am not in fact approaching death. But I am going away. I won't confuse you by attempting to explain. My first identity I established through a connection—false—to a pair of people in the partially rational City. Metal, which as you know is valueless in Paradise, is almost priceless here. With such a fortune I have done much as I liked but mostly kept to myself. The half-sanity of this second world is in some ways disturbing. I have, obviously, left a will in this place that recognizes such things, and it names you both. I am also the (spurious) uncle or guardian to many persons here, but only one might have proved an obstacle. She is a painter and will find my cash useful. You need not fear she is in your way. Probably she will drink herself to death quite soon. Her madness attracted me to her, although she is not insane in the manner of Paradise, would get no glances there."

The flirtatious lamp went out. Felion shuffled the pages of the letter and held them toward another light.

"The exit from the labyrinth is always subjective. It is controllable only by will. Maybe you won't be strong enough to operate journey's end with any skill. I must warn you, too: The labyrinth, because it is modeled on a brain, and therefore inevitably upon mine, may open randomly to show you one other particular place, or time, where I have gone, or am going. For time slips in the labryinth, and it is possible to travel into the past. I have never attempted the future, in case the future of the second city should be as dismal as the present of Paradise. You would do best to ignore these latter past excursions. The place involved would not appeal to you, although I have seen its potential and indeed, because I am insane, found it in my destiny to go there. Avoid it yourself, however—it is not for you. Keep your mind on the present parallel world I offer. The woman painter will soon die, and then you can do as you wish. You can even kill in the second city, if you want. I myself have done so, although only once. It was the day that my two introductory people became curious about me, quite suddenly, after a drinking party. On the pretense of playing with their vehicle, I destroyed something in its engine, and an hour later both of them were killed on one of the vast highways that now run over this city. I may add that in the past of the City, I have slain no one. But I believe, even so, there will be death there."

Felion skimmed through the final pages of the letter. They were repetitious and increasingly disordered.

But a little later he found the antique torches in a cupboard, and above on a shelf a box of matches, with some eccentric items, among which were two wooden dolls of Smara's, a necklace, and half a brown glass bottle with a shattered neck.

When Felion had got down to the basement and walked along the track, he reached the cavernous hall that housed the labyrinth, and now he looked at it wryly. That it should truly be the route to another world, and to other planes of time, seemed unlikely. And yet how horrifying it was, this wall of ice, shimmering, and drily wet, in the torchlight.

Like the prince in the legend, he could go in, holding up the torch, and knife in hand. (Smara should have been the priestess who stood to guard the entrance.) And in the maze, at its heart, would be a monster.

Felion listened and heard a faint roaring, like the quake of ocean captured on a screen. But it was only the blood sounding in the shells of his ears.

Suppose he went in, and it was a reality, and he could not get back? He considered Smara, alone in Paradise. In childhood, when they had begun to kill, they had formalized the slaughter, devising a ritual of changing implements. Blades, then cords, then poisons, before blades again. Of these means, Smara found the use of cords, the method of strangling, the most difficult. Generally she needed his help. And if he were not there, she might not manage the act efficiently, and die in turn.

He could burn his uncle's letter—even burn down the mansion, if necessary. Or he could merely leave at once and never come back.

But he was sane, surely, that was the whole trouble, and his sanity insisted he investigate the maze. Smara would not need to begin to kill again for some days. Even if it took him a week to return . . . And then again, would he not anyway reemerge into Paradise at the hour, minute, or moment he had left it? Pieces of the complex wandering letter had seemed to tell him this.

Felion walked across the floor, toward the white wall. It came nearer and nearer. And then he was against it. He touched the surface with his finger, and it was *cold*.

Holding the torch high, the knife in his right hand—he had been left-handed but trained himself otherwise—he entered the arched opening.

At once, everything was altered. Became absolute. Although he could still see the entry point behind him, the wall of ice towered up and up and disappeared into an indescribable nothingness above that was not mist or space—or anything.

The labyrinth was freezing, like a winter, described to Felion in bits of rotten books. The ice breathed out a faint vapor that swirled around the nasturtium tatter of the torch.

There was a smell he recognized, if only from a laboratory. Not chemical. What had it been called?

The ground was like muddied glass. (He was reminded of the shattered bottle.)

Sounds came, rushes, like seas, like ... blood moving in the ear. And he felt a slight vertigo. But then that would be proper, if the balance of matter had been disturbed.

He moved forward, following the left-hand turnings of the wall.

He believed in the labyrinth now, as he had not done when outside. He believed that it was real, and apt, and led to somewhere. His thoughts of Smara dwindled. The archway had vanished out of sight.

The first specter—hallucination, vision, element of elsewhere—spun suddenly at him, it seemed from the wall. He had not anticipated this, and despite his uncle's warning (*The labyrinth may open randomly to show you one other place or time*) had not understood what the notation might mean.

It was like a surge of the fog that clung about Paradise, but in this fog were lights, shapes, voices. Felion heard a frightful shriek, but he had grown used to shrieking. Then the sight of women was before him, ugly women and one very beautiful in a dark fur cap, or else her hair was fur. Another of the women had been struck down. She lay full-length, and the beautiful one bent abruptly to her, touching gently—and then the mirage was gone.

Felion had stopped. He shouted, "Ah! Uncle!" And then, softly, "O my prophetic soul!" And then he grinned. And saw his grinning shadow reflected from the torch into the ice wall.

Stupid to hesitate. He had had the warning and not heeded it. But the *thing* had done him no harm. No, this was not the Minotaur of the labyrinth.

Felion strode on. He whistled a tune of the bars and dives of Paradise. The walls obligingly caught it up hollowly and it echoed back to him.

The second vision came quite mildly. It was like an aperture, filling the area between the walls, the ice-rink floor, and the illimitable ceiling. He saw a dry, tawny lawn, grass, without mist, rising up to a weird house of glass. And in the glass an enormous vine was growing with bursting black fruit.

He moved toward it, and wondered for an instant, if this was the exact exit point, but certainly he had not come far enough.

And the picture smeared, crumpled, and gave way. And there the labyrinth of ice went on.

"Smara," Felion said.

He looked back. Could he *turn* back now?

Then he cursed his uncle, an awkward obscenity, for Paradise no longer had a God, a religion, or any regularized views of sexuality, to form the substance of oaths.

Felion walked on. He did not whistle.

He came around a turn, and a silver insectile web hung across the labyrinth. In the web a woman sat, her tongue protruding, and snakes for hair.

She was gone in three seconds.

And instead, he found he had reached the heart of the maze.

The heart was empty.

An oval region, with one way in from the convolutions of the ice, and a second way out.

In the floor was a stealthy mark, but it only looked as if something had scratched the surface, without intent. It was not a rune, a message, a cipher.

Felion raised the torch high again.

He recalled the woman who painted and would drink herself to death. He did not think she was one of those he had glimpsed in the hallucinatory visions. But now, standing in the womb of the ice, he credited that other world beyond, which his uncle had named, as if jestingly, *Paradis*.

Felion spent a few minutes at the core of the maze (the empty heart), and then he went on through the outleading arch, and continued, keeping to the left-hand wall.

Felion was primed now for further demons, but nothing occurred.

Nothing occurred until he came around one of the

twines of ice and saw in front of him an arch of purest nothing.

It was not like the etheric tapering-off of the ceiling. It was a sort of omission from sight. He did not like to look at it. He looked away.

Here was the end. The *egress*.

Perhaps it was all a joke. A hoax.

Perhaps the labyrinth opened into hell, whatever hell was. Or heaven. Or into colossal snows. Or the sea.

The exit could not be relied on. His will might not be able to control it.

Felion's will was strong. He and Smara had wills of iron and flame.

He glared again at the vacant arch and said aloud, "Her house. The painter who inherited from my uncle. *There.*"

And as he said it he thought, *Maybe, in this other world, there are no houses. Maybe they drift in the air—*

But the archway convulsed. It filled.

He saw a room, in shadow.

And with a howl, Felion ran between the walls, and out into that room. While as he did so, the torch puffed into darkness.

The house of the artist.

He had made it be, at the tunnel's end.

Everything about the room (he deduced it was a room) was totally uncanny to him. It was not that the furnishings and accoutrements were so alien. But no mist hung over it, and above a skylight showed rich, black night.

An easel of metal stood in the room. And elsewhere were stacked canvases, and there, a long table littered with paints, and all an artist's accessories.

He had accomplished his objective.

Felion kept still, and felt after the psyche of the house. The house of the woman who painted and drank. Who was the heir to his uncle's fortune in this other world.

And the house was like a casket, chock-full of nothing. Empty, like the labyrinth's heart.

Felion looked up.

And in the black pane of glass, he could see—*stars*.

Stars.

Felion kneeled on the floor of the studio in the parallel world of Paradis. He prayed to something that had no name.

Later, he investigated the room, but only superficially. He did not move anything from its appointed place.

When he eventually looked around for the way back into the labyrinth—this first time he was quickly satisfied, entirely overwhelmed—he could not see it.

But when he beat his head against the wall, crying, "Smara—Smara—" the wall gave way, and there it was.

As he stepped through, shuddering and hot with fear, the great cold came, and the dead torch—which all this time he had kept in one hand, the knife in the other—mysteriously revived.

He ran through the labyrinth, then. He ran through the heart of it, up against the right-hand wall.

And when he sprang out again into the cavern under the mansion of his uncle, he screamed.

Every stone reiterated his cry. He lay on the ground beside the track, hearing it, and the torch guttered out once more.

The initial killing had been a little like this. But then he had had no additional puzzlement. He had gone to Smara with a severed hand, and shown her, and they had marveled together over the whorls of its fingertips. But now, how, how to tell Smara of *this*?

FOUR

Paradis

Mary, Mary, quite contrary,
How does your garden grow?
With silver bells, and cockle shells,
And pretty maids all in a row.

Nursery Rhyme

Leocadia remained calm.

Like any sentence of death, she did not believe it.

Even after she had taken up her new life, her food and music and drink supplied, books delivered, as she wished, paints and canvas, drawing materials, notebooks, clothes, powder, everything, even then in the hermetic environ of her prison she did not believe in it. Not wholly. Not with her mind.

Was that, after all, a form of madness, then?

Even after she had sorted the pieces, grasped the plot. Accepted that her very calm itself must come from minuscule tasteless particles in her food, and in the air itself, which did not restrain her creative flair or her energy, or ability to concentrate, but which must be controlling her. Not even then.

And as she went to and fro from her room in the daylight summer hours, having found she might, and met in the corridor and garden other inmates of the Residence, who were genteel and well-mannered, sometimes bemused, excitable, but never abusive, loud, or agonized, not then either.

Until in the end even her mind knew, and it was too late, she had accepted it.

67

For, though powerless, she should have resisted. In some fashion, however oblique or useless.

Her asides to the doctors—*I'm anxious to leave, I'll tell visitors how you torture me*—were not protests or shields, let alone missiles. It was almost a repulsive flirtation, her acid quips, their smirking refutations.

And how did her life differ? She did much as she had always done. She spent a vast amount of time alone. She painted. True, the elegant dinners were gone, but had she ever really enjoyed them? True, she had no lovers, but surely it might be possible, if she were desperate, to seduce some person or other, their bizarre quality or nasty appearance offending her not at all in the onslaught of needy lust. And then again, if she could not be bothered with such unappetizing creatures, this must mean her sexuality burned low, she had had enough.

She missed walking in the City. But then, too, months had sometimes passed without her venturing more than two streets from her house.

Now she did not explore the asylum grounds. A low fence lay across the grass and trees the far side of the gravel walk, beyond the broken hothouse. It was easy to climb the fence, and now and then some inmate might scramblingly do so. But they returned from wandering among the old buildings of the madhouse disconsolate, once or twice crying.

It occurred to Leocadia that she kept the blocks of the madhouse in reserve, making of them something mystical and bad, against the ultimate rainy day of terrifying ennui.

"Oh dear, you're too late, I must go down now," Mademoiselle Varc had said to Leocadia when Leocadia first left her room and found the white woman in the corridor. "If only you had come sooner." And then she scurried to the elevator.

Leocadia then did not see Mademoiselle Varc for several weeks.

Instead she confronted Thomas the Warrior, who might once have been a wealthy old soldier, that in his youth had conceivably seen action in some small foreign war, tanks and carrier planes, and the threat of worse. Now he puffed about a flowerbed he was in charge of, below the summerhouse. It was a wonder of blooms and stone slabs, on top of one of which stood a stone head of Medusa poking out her tongue.

Thomas was elderly, thin and stooped. He paid Leocadia no attention, only speaking to his flowers. Doctor Saume had informed her of his name.

Three or four more went about the garden regularly, and some of the other older ones would bask nervously in the summerhouse. Males and females, they were sad and frequently decrepit, moaning with stiffness that even contemporary medication had not been able to alleviate.

The most immature of those she saw was a young man, possibly twenty-five years old, who crouched along like a dismembered spider. He frowned at unseen things, but meeting humans he usually brightened for a moment, telling them how well and lovely they looked. But of Leocadia he seemed afraid, and ran away and hid behind objects as she approached, even behind Thomas the Warrior and his Medusa, if nothing else were available.

Only Mademoiselle Varc actually greeted Leocadia, now thinking her her maid, her niece, her nurse, and once or twice some kind of empress or queen that she had perhaps been introduced to long ago. On these latter occasions Mademoiselle Varc curtsied, and Leocadia had felt a sudden compulsion, in case Mademoiselle Varc fell over. This was the first compassion Leocadia had ever experienced for a being other than an animal. And so Mademoiselle Varc amused Leocadia, and Leocadia was careful, in her contrary way, always to attempt to be the one she was mistaken for.

Probably the strangest time had been when Mademoiselle Varc had taken Leocadia for an old schoolfriend, and both women had then seemingly become adolescent girls. They had sat under the summerhouse in the shade of the trees, and Mademoiselle Varc had confessed she had no idea what a man and a woman did together. Leocadia had told her a carefully constrained amount, and Mademoiselle Varc had giggled girlishly, even blushed, though Dr. Duval had revealed that Mademoiselle Varc had borne six children.

When she had returned from the sun-fallen garden, kindly driven in with Mademoiselle Varc by the warden in his dark uniform (before the trees could come alive and eat them), Leocadia stepped into the dusk of her room and heard the door shut with its final click, which meant her little freedom was gone until tomorrow.

There was autonomy in the way of lamps, and she switched them on in the sitting area of the room, and going to the refrigerator, she drew out a bottle of white wine and a narrow glass.

Then she moved into the painting area and turned on the working lights.

On its easel, the picture of the ship, the beach, the spillage of oranges.

Leocadia studied it coldly.

Was it some response to the other thing upon an easel? Asra, raped and choked with orange paint, her bare flesh adorned by islands.

The doctors who had oozed charm over this painting had seen it as such; they must have done.

But she, what had she been doing?

The ship was not Asra, and yet the ship was feminine. And the sea had split her, and she. . . bled.

Leocadia drank her wine. A swirl of panic rose deep within her like a beast in a bottomless lake. How long before it would reach her surface?

She tossed the glass against the wall, where it broke. Later the wall would suck up the bits.

But not quite yet.

So interesting, the knives for her food, the glasses that might be smashed.

Leocadia went close to the painting. Yes, it could well be seen as some expression of inner horror at Asra's murder, which murder she had performed, and then forgotten.

Massed sky, the vessel with its snapped wing. And the little shells she had added. And there—what was *that?*

She leaned nearer. She could not make it out. Something white on the sand, a small distance from the shells. But not a shell.

She had not painted it. She did not know what it was.

Then again, it was done in her style, in tiny feathering brushstrokes, half its curve delineated as if cut.

Of course, they could copy her.

Leocadia crossed the room and turned about the two paintings she had previously executed here.

One a scene of a mountain, smoking over a peaceful valley. The other, a road leading into a wood. Both were dark, lowering, sinister. Neither contained a hint of orange, or any image she did not recall putting into them.

Leocadia dreamed not of distant bells but of screaming. It was full-throated and savage. It echoed and swerved through the building of the Residence. On Thomas's stone the Medusa poked out her tongue farther.

Leocadia woke up, and got out of the bed, which squeaked its incontinence plastic at her.

She went to the worktable and picked up a tube of orange paint, which she had employed without thought, as if to prove her innocence.

She uncapped it, and squeezed.

The tube screamed.

It screamed in her hand.

Leocadia kept hold of it. As her fingers relaxed, the scream stopped.

She put in on the table and pressed down on the tube with her whole hand.

Now the scream came vivid and awesome, rocking the room, dizzying her ears.

As it faded, she heard an afternote, like the boom of a massive organ in the Temple-Church twenty miles away.

Not me, Leocadia thought, concisely. It was the drugs in the food and drink, and in the light and sound and air. Or could it even be some other trick, like the orange that bled, the white ball entered in her painting?

"Or is it me?"

She seemed to stand above herself on a height, looking down into her soul, not with brief compassion, as she had gazed at the curtsying Mademoiselle Varc, but despisingly, as if at an expensive, once-reliable machine, which failed.

"Come along, Lucie," cried Mademoiselle Varc. "I've found such an interesting place. It's rather dirty, but you won't mind, will you? You're always braver than me."

Leocadia had been sitting on the hot lawn near the empty birdbath, and now Mademoiselle Varc came up and filled the bath with cold tea from her breakfast pot.

Lucie was the adolescent friend, but she and Mademoiselle Varc seemed to have grown even younger.

Leocadia was not in the mood now for role playing.

"Not today," she said, as if to a fractious infant.

But Mademoiselle Varc took no notice. She put down her alabaster hand and caught Leocadia's arm.

"Come *on*. Before they catch us."

Leocadia guessed correctly from this expression that although it was not in fact barred to them, Mademoiselle Varc wanted to go over the fence to the madhouse.

"No."

"Oh, yes. Oh do. It's really fascinating. There's all sorts of things there. I found it last week, but I didn't tell."

"No one will prevent you, if you go," said Leocadia.

"But they will. They'll spank us. It's an awful place. You know something terrible happened there. You're not scared? I dare you, Lucie."

"Of course, something terrible," said Leocadia. "What else, there?"

The old lunatic asylum. Not like the modern Residence. There had been a story about it, but then was that not the other story about the shells—that the sea had washed in over the building? No, this could never be right.

Leocadia got up as Mademoiselle Varc tugged at her like a ferocious moth.

They hurried by the summerhouse, passing Thomas the Warrior. The young spider man was creeping along and raised his face in delight to Mademoiselle Varc, saw Leocadia and lolloped away.

They rushed across the walk, and over the grass. Oak trees and gray cedar towered above them. Then there was the dilapidated fence.

It was like a boundary in a dream. But Leocadia reasoned she had perhaps already, the previous night, crossed whatever boundary there was.

Mademoiselle Varc tottered over and sat abruptly in the uncut grass the far side, but laughing.

Leocadia followed more easily.

The sun burst on the ruined hothouse and the raisin vine, black, as if mantled with bursting tarantulas.

"We have to go among the old buildings," said Mademoiselle Varc.

"Very well."

Marigolds grew wild in the long grass (and Leocadia thought of the marigolds in ice, which had prevented nothing) and pure white daisies.

Mademoiselle Varc stumbled, but she was a little girl again, only about ten, and she made nothing of it.

"Do you believe in ghosts?" she asked Leocadia. "If you look at the windows you might see them. Even by day. Women in a row."

Leocadia shrugged. She raised her eyes to the foul blank windows, seen closer now than ever before, but they were dead as ever, the optics of corpses.

Pipes thick with rust coiled from the walls of the buildings like flexible bones which had pierced the skin.

They came onto a paved place sprung with weeds. The buildings loomed above.

"This way. Down here."

Mademoiselle Varc led Leocadia toward a sort of alley between the light biscuit walls.

There was no sound. That was, one heard the sizzling chorus of cicadas, and the tweets of passing birds; insects buzzed among the rogue flowers. High, high in the sky, a plane purred almost silently over, a silver cigar with fins. All these ordinary noises. And yet, it was like the loud singing in the ear of utter soundlessness. And everything so still, as if, rather than stunned by heat, the area had been frozen.

The alley was drowned in shade.

Mademoiselle Varc darted along it in quick marsupial spasms.

Above, the ranks of corpse windows, black with grime and weather and time. From the pipes hung cakes of filth.

The alley opened in a square, around which the buildings of the madhouse reared and onto which the windows continued to stare without sight. Three big doorways seemed shut like the gates of hell.

And in the center of the square was a great heap of rubbish, stretching up five meters or more, as if constructed over some more solid base.

"See—see—" Mademoiselle Varc sprang at the garbage mountain eagerly.

Noises were fainter here, and though the sun splashed in between the roofs, it was like being in a new block of bright, thick atmosphere.

Mademoiselle scrabbled at the grisly pile.

"There!"

Leocadia observed.

She saw Mademoiselle Varc was holding up a gleaming rope of syrup, a necklace of amber beads.

How bizarre. How could such a delicacy have been overlooked? Unless Mademoiselle Varc herself had deposited them here, in order to "find" them.

Leocadia glared into the coalescence of rubble. And as she did so, she felt the eyeless windows watching, as if sudden specters had gathered behind their masks.

A pile of garbage. Old newspapers, a destroyed chair raised high as a throne. And lower down, slabs of tin and wool and corrosion.

"Look!" squeaked Mademoiselle Varc.

She raised a wooden doll with jointed arms and legs and black cotton hair.

How was she finding these things? She must have placed them here, her treasures.

"Here's another," said Mademoiselle Varc, and pointed Leocadia into the heap of debris. A wooden limb poked out, and sure enough another wooden maiden emerged into Leocadia's hands. This one had flax hair and cool glass eyes.

"I wonder what else we shall get?"

It was a festival. It was a barrel of goodies into which you must plunge your fingers.

Something was dislodged from higher up and swiveled down the rubbish with a frantic sound.

It fell at Leocadia's feet.

"Oh just see. It's given you something."

Leocadia bent down and raised the artifact.

It was an old brown bottle, curiously shaped, square, with a four-sided neck and a four-sided mouth. On the front, a label. It showed clearly a weird landscape of ice and glaciers, and before them a black and white penguin with a marigold flash beside its beak. Above, the name. *Penguin Gin*.

Leocadia examined the bottle in a trance. It was very old. It was clean, and bright. The penguin pleased her, for it was realistically portrayed, and into her head came the thought: *I have a model now. I can paint penguins.*

"Yes, I've heard of it," said Mademoiselle Varc, peering over. "There was a slogan for that gin." She held a wooden doll in either hand, the amber beads about her neck, along her whiteness. "Penguin Gin, it eases pain."

"Not in your youth, surely," said Leocadia.

"Oh no. Long before. Long, long ago."

Something shuddered in the pile of rubbish. A thin black smoke uncoiled from it.

"That's enough," cried Mademoiselle Varc. "We must go."

She sprinted back into the alley.

Leocadia turned slowly, watching the deadly walls above. Nothing was in the windows.

But she would take the bottle. She would paint penguins.

Someone knocked on the door to Leocadia's room, the way the female attendant did when she brought a hot meal.

"Yes," said Leocadia.

The door was opened.

It was eleven o'clock in the morning, and the doctors, when they came, arrived at five in the evening. Yet here was Van Orles, all alone.

"What do you want?"

"Why, to see you, mademoiselle."

Leocadia wore her cream housedress, which had so generously been sent to the asylum for her. She had no makeup on. She had been about to don her working smock and prepare a canvas.

Van Orles looked at her insidiously.

"Here I am, as you see," said Leocadia.

"Well, shall we have a little talk."

"If we must."

"Always so bristly!" merrily chided Van Orles, and he came bouncing into the room. He wore another of his pasty cravats. Sitting down on the couch he lit a pipe. Leocadia opened the second window. "You never ask for cigarishis," said Van Orles. "Don't you miss them?"

"I seldom bothered with them. They had no effect on me."

"Yet still you drink."

Leocadia propped up a canvas on her table.

"And you began to drink when you were eleven years old, I understand."

When Leocadia did not reply, Van Orles puffed away at his pipe as if considering her silence an answer.

Leocadia was irritated. She did not like to work with anyone near her, as all her lovers had soon discovered. She went to the dressing table and began to brush her curling hair with harsh strokes.

"What a lovely girl you are," murmured Van Orles. "Don't you miss other things? Companionship? Dalliance?"

A faint livid light was ominously blooming up from nowhere. She tensed. The distasteful man seemed to be making a pass at her. Leocadia swung slowly around and smiled at him. Van Orles appeared taken aback. Leocadia lifted the brown bottle off the dressing table where it had lain through the afternoon and night.

"Look at this, Where do you think I got it?"

"I've no idea."

"In a junk heap in a yard of the old building."

"Which building is that?" he inquired innocently.

"The madhouse."

"Ah. How quaint. The lunatic hospital. Really, that place should be walled off. The masonry isn't safe."

"Don't you think it's a pretty bottle?" said Leocadia. "Quite old itself, I should say, from its shape."

"Very likely." Van Orles got up carefully and came to stand over Leocadia. "And you are interested in such items?"

"Oh, yes. Why don't you tell me about the madhouse?"

"Now, we shouldn't call it that. They were awful days. The poor sick people weren't treated well. Sometimes they were even displayed to the public, to make others laugh. Immorality and disease ran rife—"

"But what happened?" said Leocadia.

"How do you mean?" Van Orles crouched closer.

Leocadia hit him quite hard on the hand and stood up. She moved away.

Van Orles looked happy. He presumably thought he was being teased, a preliminary.

"I mean," said Leocadia, "something curious took place, didn't it? The madhouse was suddenly closed down."

"Oh, there is some story—a warder was killed, and someone disappeared. Perhaps the inmates attacked the staff for their brutish treatment. But one shouldn't set too much store by tales."

Leocadia held the bottle labeled *Penguin Gin* up to the window. For a moment a screaming and contorted face seemed to writhe inside it, but it was only the action of sunlight and the shadow of ivy on the wall.

"Is that all you know, or all you'll say?" asked Leocadia.

Van Orles chuckled. He seemed to think Leocadia's prurient intriguement was a form of foreplay. Gruesome details of the lunatics might arouse her.

"There was a rumor of a ghost. A great dark thing. Very tall, gliding through the corridors. And something about a bad winter. I can't recall."

"Then," said Leocadia, "I think I'll go out for a walk."

"Now, now, not yet. I must perform a small check on your physical well-being."

Leocadia turned from her worktable, the palette knife in her hand. The glare of light was around him like a halo, the warning phenomenon that had come before.

"But I am violent," she said. "And I might not care for this small check."

"Ah—" Van Orles stepped away. He was still smiling, the smile a daisy left behind by a retreating tide. "Now, Leocadia—"

"If you touch me," said Leocadia, "if you come in here again alone, I will set on you." She was tepid, easy. She had had to threaten others. Generally they accepted her terms. And so did Van Orles.

"You are being most unreasonable, Leocadia. Merely because I can't satisfy your ghoulish curiosity about the lunatics."

"But *I'm* a lunatic," said Leocadia. "How can you trust yourself with me? What would the other doctors say if they knew?"

Leocadia walked to the door ahead of Van Orles and opened it. She went into the corridor. Van Orles stood lost in the middle of the room. Leocadia threw the knife back there, so it whirled past his head. He yelped and ducked low, and his pipe fell on the floor.

"I shall have to report this," said Van Orles.

"And also, of course, that you came to me by yourself, for how else did it happen?"

She did not want to leave him in her room, and sure enough, when she stood right back, he came hurrying out.

"You've turned nasty, Leocadia."

He hastened away.

Probably, she had been ill-advised. She was not free now, and doubtless to make such an enemy was unwise.

Outside, it was hot, the sun going up to the zenith. In the summerhouse the old ones lay like spoilt seals. Thomas was not at his garden. No one was anywhere.

Leocadia looked across the grass and gravel, between the trees to the buildings.

Cries in the night—of course. The sheer misery and abjection of that place had been recorded in its stones. But she, had she now come to the hiatus, the point where she must, even physically, pass over into her new life? The low fence symbolized this.

She could kill herself. They must mean her to, leaving all the handy knives and glasses for her. But first, there was the landscape with the penguin to paint.

Leocadia walked along the fence, not crossing it.

Large chestnut trees arose, and under their canopy she came upon the spider man sitting, looking where she looked, toward the madhouse.

Seeing her, he jumped up.

"Wait," snapped Leocadia.

He gave a wild cry. He ran, not like a spider now but a wounded hare. He rushed at the fence and sprawled across it and charged on toward the madhouse walls.

Leocadia got over the fence also, and holding up her long skirt, she ran after him grimly. Her legs were long and slim and strong; she was soon close.

"Stop," she commanded, but he shrieked and bolted away.

He chased along the paved space under the windows.

Swearing, she caught him in both hands, letting her skirt go.

He hooted, went down, and crawled at her feet.

"I won't," he said. "I won't."

"You will," she said. "Why are you afraid of me?"

"Weasel," said the young man. He touched Leocadia's sandaled foot, tore back his hand as if she burnt.

"I am not a weasel. I wish I were. Or are you supposed to be? You're a spider."

He glimpsed up at her face. He said, experimenting, "You look well today."

"I am. Tell me something about that." And she pointed at the madhouse.

"All gone," said the young man. "They went in a night. All the doors were locked. A great wave." He got up and bowed to Leocadia. "Your highness is so powerful. Do take care," he said. Then he flung himself off again, racing back at the fence, away from the buildings.

Leocadia looked up at the rows of dead windows. They were now familiar. She thought she could hear a bell ringing somewhere, but perhaps this noise was only in her ear.

The crickets were silent, and the birds. The marigolds had scorched in the grass and the daisies withered.

Gone in a night. A great wave.

Shells left behind, but that was the other story.

What had gone on here?

Leocadia turned down an alley between the buildings. It was not the way she had come with Mademoiselle Varc. Yet the alley looked just the same, the deep shade, the walls and pipes.

And sure enough, the alley led into a courtyard. Here there was a stone block. It was featureless and gave no indication of its use. Three doorways (hell gates), as before.

Leocadia crossed the yard, which had no rubbish heap, climbed a short stair, pushed at the black door. It was shut, forever.

The madhouse of Paradis.

Something fluttered on the edge of her eye.

Leocadia turned and stared up. Above, in a window, stood a feminine form with bright marmalade hair.

Leocadia's blood seemed to sink through her. A great wave . . . it hit her feet and vertigo made her drop her face into her hands. Then it was gone, and looking furiously up again, unsteady and sick, she beheld the window empty.

As she came back over the gravel, Leocadia saw Thomas the Warrior sitting under his Medusa, in the flower bed.

"Wait, mademoiselle."

"Everyone talks to me now," she said.

"You have been *there*."

"There. Where?"

"What did you see?" asked Thomas. He was elderly and gnarled and his voice was cracked.

"What could I see? Some deserted buildings."

"Once full," said Thomas the Warrior.

"Gone in a night," said Leocadia.

Did she imagine it? Was the tongue of the Medusa longer?

"You must understand. In your great-grandfather's time. The doors were all shut. The inmates packed in for the night. But in the morning, all the lunatics had gone."

He stopped. He looked like old men from her childhood. This annoyed her. She said, "Aren't we all lunatics?"

"Oh, no, mademoiselle. *You* are only mad."

"What's the difference?"

"One day you'll know. Or perhaps not."

"Tell me anyway," she said, "about the madhouse."

"They vanished," he said, "But not the warders. There were twenty of those. I can see them now—in my mind. All were found dead. Some were in corners and some pressed up against the ceiling like flies, stuck fast. Can you see it, too?"

"Dead," she said.

"Yes, mademoiselle."

"How?"

"They drowned. And they were drunk to a man. Drunk and drowned."

"But meanwhile," she said, "these may be lies. Why did you tell me?"

"You asked."

"That's no reason."

"True. I told you so that you can see all the way around the great circle, of which you are now a part. My congratulations. Now you're one of us."

"No," said Leocadia.

"Then," said Thomas, "what are you?"

He rose and came to soldierly attention as she walked away.

The new canvases were gone. That must be the doing of Van Orles, his repayment.

The rest of her equipment—paints, brushes, knives, and rags—were still there. Even the easel. Even the brown bottle with the penguin.

Penguin Gin, it eases pain.

Nothing to paint on.

Her frustration was boiling and immense.

In one of her notebooks—on the surface of which it would be impossible to apply paint—she wrote down what the spider man had said to her, and the words of Thomas. But not what she had seen in the window, the maiden with orange marmalade hair.

Penguin Gin, Penguin Gin, drink it up—

She poured vodka slowly.

The walls of the Residence seemed to be breathing. The gray screens of them must try to shift, and other barriers pass behind them, through them . . .

Beyond the window, in the sunset, the madhouse flamed.

Drunk and drowned.

She could hear the screaming, and it was night. And she knew, if she left the bed and walked to the door, it would be open. An oversight, an act of malice.

As she went across the cool floor, she was surprised that she heard the screaming still, and yet she thought, *It's not me. I'm not mad. I hear only what is.*

She went into the corridor, belting her night robe as she walked, and got to the elevator. It worked soundlessly. Had someone fixed everything just so? Was Van Orles lying in wait? And if he was, would she kill him?

But the lift went down to the garden and no one was there.

The night was soft and fragrant, without lights except for a few vague glims high up about the Residence. And the stars, sharp as pins and claws, brighter than eyes. No moon. Leocadia could not remember seeing the moon for a long while. Had it gone away from her?

She went down the lawn, the grass crisp on her bare feet, going by the birdbath with the dregs of tea. The summer-house was ghostly, the hothouse like a fiend, its vampire vine and smashed edges.

Across the grasses the ancient blocks were white now, as if after all a moon shone on them, or within. Yet the windows had stayed blind.

The fence was difficult—perhaps she had chosen a more awkward spot. It tore her robe.

Through the high grass, pleased, like a lion in the park. She got onto the paving and moved toward the alley she had taken last, and so reached the square with the stone block, and the girl phantom in the window.

Nothing now. Nevertheless, she located the particular pane, marked it out. Then she went up the steps, still warm from the summer day, and she thrust at the door.

Which opened.

Leocadia stole into the deserted halls of old madness.

She could see very clearly, a sort of night sight.

She could make out long passages, and rooms that led off them, and stairs ascending.

She did not mean to lose her way.

She chose a left-hand stair and moved up it. These steps were not warm at all. No, they were cold as marble. She shivered. And then she gazed upward.

High over the stair, high on the wall, a mark. A tide mark. Fluid had risen, and stood, and then drawn away. The wave. The wave that drowned. It had been here.

At the stairhead, she turned aside. She was going toward the place where, from the outside, she had seen the girl.

How cold, the building. How silent and—*stopped*. Like a clock that had used up all its time.

Everything was the same. Passages and doors opening into rooms. Bare, polished as bones.

And here was the one, the room that she had looked into from below.

Leocadia crossed the shining floor.

At the window, no one. And yet, the windowpane—She went near and examined it.

Upon the casement, like the play of winter frost, were two fine and narrow shapes, the prints of two hands. Formed in ice. A little moisture trickled from them, but only a very little.

If I'm dreaming, I can wake up now.

But she could not.

The cries and screams had faded. There were only the handprints and the print of high tide on the walls, and the freezing stillness out of time.

She left the room quickly. She ran toward the stair and rushed down it. Fear had almost caught her up. Below too she ran, for the doorway, and dashed through it and down the steps.

Too cold.

Up the alley Leocadia flew. It was as if the madhouse might collapse on her, masonry unsafe—

She grazed her feet on the paving, and among the long grasses she fell once but jumped up and ran on.

As she managed the fence, she felt her heart beating pitilessly.

The gravel hurt. It was hot now, after the coldness. She entered the Residence and found the elevator, and it went up with her, up and up, and it took too long, but here was the corridor, so modern and pristine, without the marks of tides. She came to her room, and the door gave without fuss. She closed herself in. She stumbled to her bed, and as she lay down on it, she woke up.

Her eyes opened. She was stretched out full-length. She had been dreaming, then. But she was so cold, so chilled.

She pushed herself off the bed, and stepped over her night robe, which was lying on the floor, with a tear in it. Her feet were sore, yet numb. She got to the door and tried it—fast shut. She had never been out.

Leocadia went into the alcove with the refrigerator. Shivering with cold, she wanted a drink, the revitalizing vodka.

She opened the refrigerator. A gust of delicious warmth poured out on her.

She saw the ice packed in, but like feathers from some glorious bed. She touched it. It was soothing, smooth, like the stone hot-water bottles that had come back into fashion. It gave off heat.

She took out and poured the vodka. Cold, as it was meant to be.

She stood by the refrigerator for warmth. It was wonderful, like a summer meadow.

She turned, to warm her back in its depths, and saw across the room a great shadow. Over two meters in height, like a black column with an aproned core of whiteness. Its elongate and fearful head was moving. Horizontal, elliptical. Daggered.

The glass dropped from Leocadia's hand, and as it broke, she touched the light switch beside the alcove.

The lights roared on. She could not see. And then she did, and the room was empty. The night was warm and the refrigerator cold. Her feet were not sore.

But across the floor, she could still see it, the tear in her night robe the fence had made.

FIVE

Paradys

■

Georgie Porgie, Pudding and Pie,
Kissed the girls and made them cry.

Nursery Rhyme

"Very well, you may go. Anything to shake you out of this silly mood."

So Madame Koster pronounced, hearing that Hilde was to go over to spend the afternoon with Angeline. Madame did not inquire into this. She was drawn and ill-tempered, had headaches. Normally she would have asked to see the invitation.

Hilde went in the Koster carriage.

Let off at Angeline's house, she loitered until the carriage was gone. Then she found her way, with some difficulty, but with the glow of purpose on her, to the street of the large theater.

She had not thought any of her adventure through. Had not considered that one day, conversing, her mama might mention to Angeline's mama the afternoon the two girls had been together. But then, what did that matter?

Hilde approached the theater diffidently but proudly. She had the pride of youngness, and its abashment, too.

There was an old doorkeeper by the actors' entrance.

"What can I do for you, mademoiselle?"

"Monsieur Martin—" Even to pronounce his name was like a stab of fire to her.

"That's right, mademoiselle. But there's no performance. Not until later tonight."

"I have a packet for Monsieur Martin."

Hilde did not really grasp from where her invention had come. Some novel? But there it was. And, oddly, the doorkeeper responded. Not by asking after the packet (for example where was it?) but by looking at Hilde cunningly and crudely.

"Yes? Well, monsieur never said. Remiss of monsieur."

"I must see him," said Hilde, one minute a flame, and then the white of ice.

"Yes. Well. Monsieur does see a lady now and then. But usually," the doorkeeper rapped his coat.

Hilde did not know why. She, or her actor, should have tipped the old man, this overseer of indiscretions.

"I must—" repeated Hilde.

"Yes, yes. He's there. Go in, then." The overseer spat past Hilde's pretty skirt. "I suppose he'll settle. Later. Or not. But then, mustn't speak ill of *Monsieur*. Oh, no. Up you go. Up all the stairs, then left at the top. Perhaps he'll be waiting."

Hilde did not comprehend any of it, not even that *Monsieur saw ladies*. She did not know, of course, that Martin had come for some adjustment of costume, and that, liking his dressing room for its ambience—the cloister of the cathedral of art—he sometimes lounged about there, looking over his lines and exquisitely twisting them, pacing around and smoking. It was not often that a woman had come there to him, but once, or twice, they had.

Now Hilde climbed the horrible stone stairs, on which lay cigarette corpses, flakes of broken glass, dead flowers, clouded stains— all the evidence of vile prediction. But why should she guess?

As she rose a smell grew more dense. It was of the greasepaints the actors used and the creams whereby they got them off, also of dusty clothes that somehow stank of the history they faked. And there was alcohol and tobacco, and the incense of inner things. It *was* a church, in its way.

Half there, Hilde felt faint and leaned on the wall. But then she braced herself. She too was holy. Possibly it was some emanation of his that had made her into an acolyte. He had not meant it to.

She reached the top of the dark tower.

There had been other corridors, but here was one that was black even in daylight. Had she been older, some intimation of death might have held her back. But she had too recently come the other way. She did not identify.

Hilde walked softly into the corridor and so, as if in some dream, came to a line of doors.

She moved down them, lost. And in that second two men rolled from a corner wheeling a costume hamper between them. They stared at her, and so she said, "Monsieur Martin?" Her password.

One of the men grinned. He directed her. It *was* the helpfulness of the spider in the web: *This way*.

When she had gone, he turned to his mate. "That worm. He gets it all. Nice young bit like that."

"Maybe his sister."

"Oh, for *sure*."

As Hilde went between the doors and so reached the proper one, the hamper descended to the enormous wings of the stage, where it was left. Here the hollow cutouts of scenery rested like vampirized dinosaurs, and ropes and pulleys, chains and spars were stranded, as if on the decks of a ship.

Cleaners had been sweeping the stage.

"Johan has a girl again," said one of the descended men.

"Poor bitch. What do they see in the bugger?"

"Why, he's an actor," said one of the sweepers, striking a pose with his broom. "Glamour. That means magic."

Storeys up, Hilde knocked on the door.

His beautiful voice (it was beautiful) spoke brusquely. "Yes? What?"

She could not speak, could not, for her life.

But soon, half angry at being disturbed in his meditations, he flung the door open.

So he noticed her again. And she him.

"Yes? What do you want?"

She gazed at him. Speech, strangely, came.

"To find you."

"Oh, very well. What is it?"

But then, but then, he *saw* her once more.

He saw her now as a woman, though young as a new moon. He saw her as lovely—that is, *attracting*. He saw that she was there. Some vague remembrance arrived, too. She was an abject subject of his, a convert. Some well-off sempstress of the streets, probably, who had stitched her fine dress herself and put it on to impress him, for who else would seek him in this way?

And she was charming. Skin like lilies, hair like apricots. Eyes cast down. And trembling.

His art fired him also, Johanos. It aroused him, and he had been viewing his art, here in the cramped room with its piles of stale clothes, and cluttered screens, and a bottle of brandy, and cigarettes, and manuscript, and *his spirit* crammed in everywhere. The room that led to the high altar.

Not merely acolyte. Sacrifice.

Down on the stage a mile beneath, the cleaners were mock fighting, being the Roman and his Foe, with brooms. Blobs of dust and waves of sawdust were stirred, it was like the parting of a sea. And behind stood the movable walls of the scenes, a hundred countries, other worlds.

But Johanos Martin said to Hilde, "Yes, I understand. Come in."

And as she entered his cell, the priest took her between his hands.

Hilde looked up at him. She could not see the error for the exactitude.

"Johanos—" she said.

"Oh, are we on familiar terms? Perhaps we are."

He did not admit though, that, this being the case, he had forgotten. He bent his head and kissed her lightly and Hilde slid against him, becoming only soul, dissolving.

So then he kissed her more deeply, this offering. She was fragrant and delicious. Obviously, one must have more.

To Hilde it was the dream come true. It was the truth, reality.

Below on the stage one broomer stabbed the other. Handle jutting out beneath his armpit, this other howled. "Oh! I die! I die! What cities and what lands fall down with me."

"Bastard," said an other, "I'll take my bet he's dying on her now."

He had drawn her to the rickety little couch and there undone her bodice and slipped in his hands. She cried now with shame and pleasure. He had never had a girl so young, took her for seventeen, pulled up her skirt and touched between her melting thighs.

She did not know anything beyond his touch. She had given herself over to the service of the high altar. She was the sacrifice. He wanted her and by some extreme telepathy had extended his need to her innermost mind.

One of the broom men fell "dead." The other straddled him, and then all looked up into the soaring flies.

They cursed Johanos Martin, whom they hated, for he was stingy and rude, imperious, mean, and frozen like old winter.

And just then he thrust into Hilde's body, tearing her so she screamed with shock and hurt and some mad outrage that was not only of the flesh.

She tried to fight him off. He struck her white face, leaving a lurid mark that faded quickly, for he had not, gentleman that he was, struck very hard.

He finished in twenty seconds. A breach, a ramming motion, the explosion of a passion cold as heat.

"Silly girl," he said, getting up, turning his back, adjusting his male dignity. "I'm sorry I was rough. But you shouldn't entice and then be coy. We've done it before." Even her virginity had gone for nothing. He thought her tight and awkward from inexperience and perversity.

Hilde, too, somehow got to her feet. She stood, drooping, almost bent right forward, like a snapped stem.

Up the stairs a cleaner boy was running. He was bringing Johanos Martin the Hated a gift from the street, but Hilde did not know.

"What have you done?" she said.

"Oh, come now."

"Why have you done this to me—"

"Now, don't be stupid. For God's sake. You'll be asking for money next."

Hilde straighened wearily. She was in pain, as if she had given birth. She had. The birth of terror.

"Please, help me," she said. For in this Ultima Thule of life, still she looked to him, her lover, to offer her hope and help.

But Johanos Martin was disgusted.

"For God's sake, get out. How can I deal with this? Get out, you little whore, or I'll send for the police."

Hilde was numb, and now speechless again. She had entered the world of nightmare, which she would never leave. Or not until another nightmare woke her. Despair had occurred suddenly. As such things do.

She tidied her clothes reflexively, and went to the door, which he was now theatrically holding open for her. As she went forth, the door banged.

So she saw and smelled, outside in the corridor, the shovelful of horse's dung collected for him from the street, and spread out carefully on the ground.

She was beyond fainting, as the starving man is beyond hunger. There were no escapes.

She stepped over the dung and slowly went down through the building.

She would never afterward remember doing so, only the reek of the feces of a grass-eating animal, fed on stuff that was not natural to it.

In a country that has no justice and logic, it is useless to behave normally. Hilde did try. In the nightmare world, she attempted to sleep, to get up, to eat, to dress herself and go about with her mother on the endless trivial errands of their

92

house. But Hilde was passionate. It had been kept closed up in her the way a flower is closed in a bud. Once open it can only bloom and blow, and then the petals fall. The fall had come.

Hilde did not sleep. She wept all night and rent the sheets and bit the pillows from agony. Her maid saw what had happened to the linen and told madame, and madame shouted at Hilde. Was she a wild animal from the zoo?

Hilde did not, and perhaps could not, say what was wrong with her. Neither could she swallow food. She found it impossible to get up from her bed. If forced to do so, she sat in her robe before the mirror, unable to proceed further.

She stared at herself. Who was this?

She had hidden the doll in the wardrobe, that it might not see.

And God—Hilde called to Him but He had not regained His hearing.

The doctor was fetched instead. He said these foolish vapors afflicted young girls, and prescribed a tonic, rest, and exercise. Hilde drank the tonic, which tasted of hot iron. Her mother drove her out, accompanied by the bored and resentful maid, to walk in the parks of Paradys.

Hilde began to suffer from fits of searing rage. She flung a bottle of cologne across her room and it broke. Sometimes she would stand before her mirror and shriek at herself wordlessly.

Her father spoke sternly to Hilde. Hilde sat before him like a dead doll.

Hilde's mother shouted at Hilde and slapped her hands with a narrow silver bookmark. Hilde started to wail and cry.

The truth was expelled from Hilde by the tiny irritant pain of the bookmark on her knuckles, one last straw.

"I can't bear it—I can't! I love him. There's nothing else. He—he killed me."

"What? Who? What are you talking about, you uncontrolled and wretched girl?"

"Johanos—" said Hilde. And at the name, the fissure was soldered shut again. It had let out everything that was necessary.

And now Madame Koster slapped her daughter across the face, as Martin the priest had done.

"What a lying little beast. Are you mad? You've seen him only once, in this house. These idiotic fanstasies. Such a man is far beyond you. And besides, unsuitable. A common actor. Don't let your father hear a word of this."

But Hilde turned and ran about the room, up and down, like a dog in a cage. She beat the walls with her fists, and her cries were so loud now they might be heard in the street.

Her mother rushed at her and slapped her hard again, two or three times, until Hilde fell on the floor.

"How can I live?" said Hilde. Her words were unintelligible. "How can I bear it?" She was, of course, too young to know that much of life involves the bearing of what cannot and should not be borne.

And Madame Koster, who did know, being seasoned enough, and who had the passion of a small gnat in her heart, imagined that her self-control was due to her superior type, and that Hilde's lack of it was proof of Hilde's revolting weakness and unworthiness. As Hilde lay there, madame her mother would have kicked her. For being all madame was not. Therefore an insult, a challenge, and a threat.

All love was gone. Dream love, and motherly love.

Hilde was locked into her room, where she lay in a stupor, not caring.

And then madame brooded. And presently she summoned her husband home.

The Koster house was built of respectability, of reasonable sane ambitions, formats and rites. Hilde was a spy of chaos who had got in, masquerading as a daughter.

Two doctors tested Hilde's mind carefully. They conferred with monsieur. Madame shed a few dryish tears.

Only thirteen days had passed since Hilde's return from the Goddess of Tragedy.

94

"It seems she is the victim of—monsieur, forgive me—a sexual delusion and a frenzy. It affects certain unlucky young women in this way. Such women are feeble, unformed. They are not meant for physical ardor and can't withstand it. The proper female votive of sacrifice and tenderness becomes warped into obsession. She's a danger to herself, and to others."

The Kosters had put it about that their daughter was gravely ill, and when word came that she had abruptly died, there was speculation but no disbelief. Death did descend in this way, and the young were vulnerable. That the parents were secretive and sorrowful was only to be expected. The funeral was very private, indeed, clandestine.

A headstone appeared in the graveyeard. Those who discovered and read it were sometimes struck that it was a little odd. "Our dear daughter, Hilde, strayed from our lives . . ."

Massively drugged, insensible, Hilde was taken away in a closed carriage at three in the morning. It was all managed very discreetly. If people saw, they did not understand.

The carriage wheeled sedately through Paradys, along the cobbled lanes and up the wide paved roads, under the churches. Our Lady of Sighs, Our Lady of Smokes. Beneath the Temple-Church. Reflected in the river. It went up into the hills to where the last of the dark trees were, beyond the outlying architecture of the City, and came to a big brick citadel, sometime before dawn.

The walls were high, the gate was straight.

It was the lunatic asylum of Paradys. The madhouse.

The door slammed shut again, on Hilde.

SIX

Paradise

▲

We are outside the Labryinth now. Searching,
only finding. Staring headlong into a ghost's
looking-glass.

John Kaiine

In the garden room of her apartment, Smara had been
working the clockwork cat. The clockwork, however, was
wearing out, and the cat was no longer friendly, as it had
been in Felion's and Smara's youth. It would pad a few
meters, and then stop.

The garden room had plants made of black velvet and
rubber, and sometimes Smara dusted them. Their mother
had spent many hours here, before one day she flung herself
off a high tower in the City. Their father was unknown to
them.

When Felion arrived, they drank sweet wine and talked
about ordinary things. Smara had killed a woman in a
cemetery, managing to lasso her as she knelt over a grave.

Finally, Smara said, "But you went into the labyrinth,
didn't you?"

"Yes. Shall I tell you?"

"If you want," said Smara. Her face was sharp and anxious.

Felion told her what he had seen in the passages of the
ice, the visions of women, the glass building, the being in the
web. He spoke of the empty heart at the labyrinth's center,
and how nothing disturbed him on the farther side, until he
emerged into the studio of the artist their uncle had made
his inheritrix.

Smara listened, but she kept moving about. She began to dust the plants, and the stone head that stood on a plinth against one window.

"And will you go back?" she inquired when he had ended.

"I think I will. There were stars, I saw them, Smara, through a skylight. The sky was a deep black, and there they were. I want you to see them too. And the sun. And the moon."

"Oh, but I've seen that," she said. "In pictures."

Felion began to persuade her, to nag her and wear her down.

She allowed him to talk, but soon she got up and wandered from the room, and so from room to room of the apartment. Felion pursued her, still talking, nagging.

It grew dark, and the opaque gray blanks of the windows changed to ebony. Sometimes a light might shine out there from some height or other, and tonight there was one, quite fierce, and fluctuating. Probably something was on fire.

Felion was hoarse. He left off and only sat looking at Smara. There was nothing to eat in the apartment.

"Shall we go out and find some food?"

But now Smara said, "Why must I come into the labyrinth?"

"To reach the other city."

"Is it so wonderful, then?"

"It must be." He added, "You mustn't be afraid of the ice. It's not like winter." This was a lie. "And I'd be with you."

She did not reply then, but as they walked the wide smoggy streets, she said, "I've been thinking of it, the other city." Then, as they ate burned potatoes in a café, she found a round rock, of course, cooked in with the vegetables. She said, "I asked for bread, and into my hand was put a stone."

Felion flung the rock at the cook, who had appeared in the café. The man shied, laughing, and the rock only broke another window.

"We can go tonight," said Smara. "Yes, I'll try."

He took her right hand at the entrance. In her left he had seen she carried her killing cord. He held up the torch, and the ice wall gleamed.

She looked frightened, but she did not hold back now.

They went in together. They were inside.

Then they walked forward, keeping to the left, not speaking.

The sounds came, the dim roar like oceans. Smara made no comment, asked no questions. Her hand felt as cold as the ice.

Felion waited for the visions, but nothing stirred.

Suddenly Smara said, "Oh, look!"

But Felion could see nothing at all.

"What is it? I don't—"

"That old man in a garden ... Isn't it our uncle? He's dressed as he was in the photograph, the one taken during the war. And look—oh, *look!* There are flowers—just like the ones the screens show."

Felion could make out nothing, but Smara's white face was alight with interest. Then she blinked. "It's gone."

"I didn't see. But it must be one of the elements he said we'd find here—time slips, images of some other place. He said he went there, as well as to the city. He went there or would be going there... And so. Probably you saw him."

"There was a glass building," she said. "It had white and brownish panes."

They went on. Smara moved quickly now.

No images unfolded before Felion, and Smara apparently saw nothing else. Quite swiftly, they reached the center.

Inside this icy oval, Smara hesitated.

She stared about her, and drew her right hand from Felion's grasp.

"This is a terrible spot," she said. *"Something's here."*

"No, nothing at all. It's empty."

"Yes, there is something. Something horrible and dangerous."

"No." Felion put his head on her shoulder.

Smara darted her head upward and pointed, into the height of the ice wall.

And something was there. A kind of hump bulging out in the ice. It had not been present before.

He said, "Smara, you must control yourself. You're making this happen. It's *you*."

She covered her eyes with her hands.

The bulge in the ice did not go away, but it had now a fixed, inert appearance.

"How much further?" Smara whispered.

"I don't know. Not far."

All at once she broke from him and ran off.

He shouted after her, and also ran to catch her up, but although in the City he could have done this easily, here something prevented him. And so she was gone, flying ahead, vanishing. He called that she must keep to the left of the walls. He remembered how he had told her over and over that will had projected him through into the second world, and where they would be going: the studio of the woman artist.

Then, running, he reached the exit point, and saw, with hardly any forethought, the studio outside.

He rushed into it—but Smara was not there.

Again, as before, the house in the second world was vacant.

At first, he barely noticed, searching about in it, uncaring and unthinking, for his sister. Who mattered, what counted, but she?

But Felion did not find Smara.

Instead, he found other things.

The rooms were quaint, some orderly and clean, others jumbled. Dead flowers (flowers!) in a vase, the butts of cigarettes with a scented smell, books—intact—cast about lying on the carpets. There were glasses with the phantoms of alcoholic perfume, but no dregs.

On the walls hung interesting pictures. There were persons in them with the heads of beasts Felion recognized from the screens and portions of books in Paradise.

The furnishings were not so dissimilar to those he knew. That was a chair, and this a table, a cupboard, an ashtray, a cup.

But.

The windows.

It was dawn, he thought, and he saw a sun come up. It was an orb like a lamp, but quickly it became too bright to regard. Then the whole sky flooded with brilliance and color.

Did Smara see this? Where was she?

He hunted through the house of windows, and piece by piece the strangeness, the volume, of what he saw overcame even his concern for Smara.

He did not leave the building. And yet, outside, he beheld streets. There were old trees, growing and real. It was possible to see a long way, because there was no mist.

Felion wondered, if anyone entered the house, what he would do. But no one came to the house, and outside the calmest day went by. Vehicles passed now and then, and sometimes people walked along, in costumes that, as with the furniture, were not so unlike the clothing of Paradise, although he noticed no masks.

He could not find a cooking area, or anywhere to come on a drink; he longed for water. There seemed to be mechanisms that worked for the maintenance of the house, but he could not activate them, for the panels that apparently related to them were incomprehensible.

In the hallway at the bottom of the house there was some evidence of the passage of many people. He noticed that something had been done to the door, externally, which worked to secure it. A spangled woman's shoe lay on the stair.

The day went with the passage of its sun, and bars of light and shadow roamed over the chambers, fascinating him. The whole house was like a clock.

At length, he went back to the upper attic room, the painter's room.

He realized now, something seemed to have happened here, too. He was uncertain what. Some tubes of paint were stuck to the floor. With distaste, he found that someone had vomited in a corner.

As previously, the exit-entry point had disappeared, and in a sudden rage he crashed his fist against the wall.

"Let me through. I want Smara."

It was what they had called *dusk*. He could hardly believe he had spent so much time here, when she—

The wall gave way. It was as much emotion, then, as will that caused the labyrinth to operate.

The tunnel of ice curled before him, and idiotically he glanced at the ground, to see if Smara had left lying there one of her shoes, to guide him. But there was nothing.

He stared around the attic again. He had looked at some of the canvases that were stacked against the wall. One had a blond man standing on a roof, high above a city that was devoid of mist.

Inside the maze, he walked backward, watching the aperture, until it abruptly dissolved.

As he came into the center of the labyrinth, Felion paused.

His heart beat heavily; he was conscious of great fatigue and mental enervation.

It was now incredible to him he had lingered so long in the parallel house of a painter (whose name his uncle had never bothered to tell him) when his sister had vanished inside the maze of ice.

He looked up, and there the bulge still was, in the ice wall. It had changed.

Above, the ice had sunk to a type of darkness, almost like some view of the misty night of Paradise. And in the space thus supplied, the frozen tumor had gone to a blocked and incoherent shape. But it was tall, and had a birdlike head—

In that moment, Felion heard light footsteps on the floor of the ice, tapping toward him. His blood leapt, he looked down, and saw Smara.

She stepped into the heart of the maze nearly indifferently. She was not pale, but nearly luminous, as he had seen her after a particularly fortuitous murder.

She too looked at him, and stopped.

"Here you are," she said.

"You ran away," he said. "Where did you go?"

"Into the painter's studio, where else?"

"But—I was there. I explored the house. I didn't find you."

"Nor I you." She frowned. "Somehow that seemed to be all right. I knew I'd find you *here*."

"We must," he said, "have gone into the studio on different planes of time. Did you see her, then?"

"No, The room was empty."

"What hour of day was it?" he asked. He trembled with relief at discovering her, did not mind what they said, or where they were.

"Day, I think. There was *sunlight*. It fell across the floor from the two windows."

"The window in the roof?"

"No, one in each wall. One gave on a bank of vines. The other window had a view. A lawn and trees, some buildings . . ."

"We weren't in the same place," he said.

Smara scowled, as if he had accused her of some misdemeanor, as had sometimes happened in their childhood. "It was her studio," said Smara. "There was an easel with a painting on it."

"Of what?" he asked darkly.

"A ship," said Smara.

"Do you recognize a ship?"

". . . Yes, from a picture. It had a sail. Things were spilling out of it. I don't know what."

"The bitch must have two studios. What did you do in this room?"

"Very little. I was only there a few minutes. Then I came back to look for you."

"How?"

Smara lowered her eyes. She seemed angry also. "I cried out your name at the wall. I'd got in there."

Felion swept his arm upward.

"What's that?"

Smara glanced. She became pale again and distressed. "I didn't do it."

"It's your fear. It's some sort of bird of ice. It's formed itself there."

"I won't stay here," she said. She was immobile.

He went to her and took her hand. She still held, limply, her strangler's cord.

"We'll go back, then."

They walked away into the convolutions of the labyrinth. He said, "Don't be afraid of birds."

"You used to flap with the sheet and say—"

"I was horrible. Please forgive me and forget it. We were only seven."

"I saw the picture of a bird once. It was black and white. It had a terrible beak."

"I looked for it in the books," he said, "specially. It was a totem of the peoples of the northern ice waste. A spirit fashioned as a bird, with a black head and a white breast. And it was a good spirit, which they invoked to bring them help. It cured the sick."

"Are you pretending?" she questioned.

No visions came, the ice walls slid curving around them. They did not run.

"It's true," said Felion.

"In her room" Smara said, "I did something."

"What?"

"Will it hurt?" she said.

"I don't know. Damn her, who is she? Who cares?"

"I painted in something white on her picture. I don't know why. A ball of ice."

"How?" he said, again, curious and unnerved. He had done nothing.

"One of the brushes you gave me," she said, "from the man you killed. I had it with me. I used her paint. It was as if I'd always meant to, and—"

"Yes?" he said.

"I hid her spare canvases. The ones she hadn't used."

"Why?"

"I don't know. I hate her. She lives *there*."

In the winds of the ice, he turned his sister toward him and kissed her forehead.

"Forget her," he said. "Then she won't be in our way. Did you like the sun?"

"Yes."

"Wait," he said, "until we see the moon by night."

Smara had shut herself into her apartment. Felion knew that she was there, although she would not answer his signal at the door. She had not been out for days, save for one night when, turning into her street, he saw her gliding up the steps of her home. By the time he had reached it, she was inside.

He too killed desultorily, with the strangler's noose. But he was not interested in the activity now.

The idea of the labyrinth, and the city beyond, had come to obsess him.

He thought about the parallel endlessly, visualizing for himself how it might look, its heights and depths, its river—for surely, like Paradise, it had one.

His own room was in a hovel. He preferred this, he disliked possessions, for they seemed to gain a hold over him. To the clockwork cat, for example, he had had a loyalty, insisting on trying to make it work, to carry out its old antics of play and purring. But the cat was stubborn. It had "died." Smara only used its leftovers for a distraction, it did not disturb her.

In Felion's room, which was in a ruined building near a quay once known as Angel, Felion kept a hammock to sleep in and a steel safe in which lay his weapons, a few fragmented books, and some clothes. Across the door, which was itself off its hinges, stretched an electrical device that kept out intruders. One day, probably, this too would break.

Felion stayed in his room or walked by the river.

Gigantic rats, quite beautiful, but savage, prowled the edges of the water. Sometimes Felion fed them with parts of bodies, but not often. He did not want the rats to become a responsibility.

After two weeks, when Smara was still locked away, he returned to his uncle's labyrinth.

As he walked forward, he counted the turns of the ice wall. He was just inside the fifth turning when the first vision appeared.

Felion stopped, staring.

Like Smara, or as Smara had claimed it, it seemed to him he saw his uncle. But not in a garden. The old man was shambling through an alley, an alley of the elsewhere place, with no mist, and only a light on him that came down from the sky. Felion looked up, and so he saw it, the moon by night.

It was the moon—round as the perfection of all circles, russet as parchment, *bright*—it was the moon, not his uncle, that pulled Felion into the vision.

And the image did not burst or fade. It stayed whole about him.

He was brave, blasé. He thought, *I can get back, in and out as I want. I'm somewhere he told me not to go. So what?*

Felion followed his uncle along the alley in the moonlight, and so up onto higher ground.

It seemed to Felion his uncle was younger, but that might only be an effect of the amazing darkness. Felion heard his uncle's feet on the cobbles and in slicks of mud. Heard his *own* footfalls. . . . But the uncle of Felion did not turn. He seemed, the uncle, immersed in some dream, now and then gazing up at the moon. Just as Felion did.

Smara, you should have seen— you will see.

There was a bar or drinking shop up the slope beyond the alley, and Felion's uncle went in there. Felion stalled. Then he, too, made to go in. There was a sign hung over the door: A half-transparent figure hurried over a hill, under which was a rim of light; a ghost fleeing the dawn, as in Paradise, maybe, it would not have to? On a wall in the picture curled something with the black head of a bird.

Felion did not understand this sign, nor the writing beneath. The letters of it were like those of Paradise, but not the language. His uncle had not warned him that in Parad*is* they would have to learn to speak a foreign tongue.

Inside the bar, under the beams, Felion's uncle sat drinking and writing on a tablet of paper.

The clothing of the people here was not quite like the garments Felion had glimpsed from the artist's house. It was, evidently, a different time.

From another table, a gang of evil-looking humans raised their glasses to Felion's uncle.

"Here's health to you, poet!"

Felion withdrew, back into the street.

In the alley a women was selling herself to a man. As Felion went by, she smiled at him, over her customer's bowed skull. "Only wait a moment."

It came to him that after all he understood their speech, only their writing was incomprehensible.

Felion reached the end of the alley, and walked back, as he meant to, into the labyrinth of ice.

How easy. He must assure Smara again of how straightforward the adventure was.

No other visions come.

He reached the heart.

He made himself look up, and there that bird thing was, still shaped out of the ice.

Across the murky floor had been scattered some scraps of brown sugar, or glass.

Felion turned around. He did not want to go on without his sister. He would have to bully her again. He wanted her to see the moon.

He walked back out of the maze, and nothing happened. It was as if he had cheated or mocked it, and he expected trouble, but there was none.

Below the hundred steps leading to his uncle's house, Felion found a woman and, with a kind word, strangled her abruptly. He took her earrings of pearl for his sister and put them through the receptor of her door, impatiently, when still she would not let him in.

A day after, they met by accident in the nave of the cathedral. No one else was there but for a corpse lying in a side chapel, unknown by sight to either of them.

"Come back into the other city."

"I went there," she said, "in a dream."

"That isn't the same," he said.

Smara shook her head sternly. "How can we know? I saw *her* studio again, by night. I was outside and I opened the door. Someone was sleeping there, but I didn't go in. I stayed outside. There was an elevator. . . . Downstairs there were lawns and tall trees. In a lighted window was a man peering out at me. I ran back again. There was," she added, "a house of glass with a vine of fruit in it. But the vine was dead and the glass had broken."

"Was the glass brown?" he said.

"I don't think it was."

"Come with me," he said.

Smara said, "Not today. Not yet."

SEVEN

Paradis

●

The north wind doth blow,
And we shall have snow.

Nursery Rhyme

Hot summer light: The room seemed arid, and larger than
before, and Leocadia sat with her robe across her lap, examining the tear at its hem. She must have got out of the bed
and wandered around the chamber, and caught the silk on
something. On what? Some shred of broken glass the mechanical device had not cleared? (During the night the
second broken glass had also been cleared up, the glass she
had dropped when she saw a black pillar with a beaked
dagger of head standing there across the room.)

The panel that supplied music and told the time had also
a small button to summon the attendant.

Summoned, the girl in the dark uniform now knocked
and entered. It was always the same girl. Or could it be that
they simply employed a number of girls who closely resembled each other, sisters perhaps?

"Yes, mademoiselle? Would you like a cooked breakfast?
There are some excellent rolls, just made—"

"No, I don't want breakfast. I want to see one of the
doctors."

"I understand, mademoiselle. Are you feeling worse?"

"Worse. You mean, I'm always ill, so now I must be
worse. I'm neither. Duval will do. Or Leibiche. Even Saume,
probably. *Not* Van Orles."

The maid—one thought of her as a maid, rather than a jailor—smiled. "Very well, mademoiselle. I'll take your message. But I can't promise anything. The doctors are always very busy."

When she was gone, Leocadia went to her refrigerator. She opened it quickly. Chill air smoked out, winter in little.

Last night the refrigerator had been warm and she had basked against it.

Now she poured out vodka, and drew forth a long sliver of white cheese.

If the temperature of the refrigerator had failed, the food would be spoiled, and it was not.

Had she still been dreaming? The warmth, the apparition? No, for another of the glasses was missing, the one she had dropped in startlement.

Leocadia glanced aside. Nothing was disturbed, no shards of glass on the floor. Her canvases, removed by Van Orles when she was out, were still missing.

He must be amused, gratified. All her painting materials left to her, and no means for their use. Of course, even such a fool would know what this would do to her.

If one of the other doctors came, doubtless he would have been told Leocadia herself had demanded the subtraction of the canvases, or made some threat having to do with them. It would be unwise to accuse Van Orles of anything, let alone report his graceless lechery.

How many, trapped here, had submitted, to him or to some other? And would she have to prostitute herself to get her canvases back? After all, anything could be taken away from her, a reason could always be found, since she was insane.

All afternoon, no one had visited. Nor at five o'clock, the usual time.

Leocadia went down into the garden.

No one was there, either.

The summerhouse and flower bed, empty. A pigeon flew away from the Medusa's head at Leocadia's approach.

The lawns and walk were vacant, and across the grass, through the trees, the buildings of the madhouse were like old rocks in a desert.

Penguin Gin, Leocadia thought, *Penguin Gin. Drink it up, it will—*

Leocadia could not recall, out in the garden, where she had left the antique bottle with its square neck and top, its label of ice floes and bird.

She felt almost afrighted, a kind of pang.

Leocadia made herself move slowly back toward the Residence—someone might be watching.

When she gained her room, the bottle was standing on her worktable. Had she put it there? Had it been there all the time?

Leocadia picked up the bottle and examined it, an archaeologist with a flask of Egyptian pottery, some tiny god incised upon it.

Drink it up, it will—

Maddening, a rhyme that did not conclude.

Maddening.

Of course, possibly they watched her in her room, in the same way that unseen sounds and unheard lights threaded through it. But then again, if they had decided to keep clear of her—some campaign of theirs, or else some ploy of *his*—probably they would monitor her response but not interfere.

She felt a consoling violence as she prepared the wall beyond the book alcove.

The best of the light fell here, almost as good as the spot where the easel balanced.

There would be difficulties, but they must be met in the nature of challenges rather than of barriers.

The walls had always annoyed her. The pale gray surfaces without texture, against which she saw the motes in her eyes.

To change the wall, smother it in shadows and densities, illusions and images, that was a fair return.

And whatever else, unlike canvas and oiled paper, the plaster, the bricks and mortar, could not be taken away from her.

She covered a large area, larger than any canvas she had ever attempted.

Then, leaving it to dry, she took the gin bottle to the ivy window and studied it again.

The next day, Leocadia walked around the asylum grounds and across to the old buildings.

She patrolled their alleys and looked up at their windows. She paused in their courtyards, listening.

She did not come on the great teetering rubbish tip— either it had vanished, or she had chosen the wrong entry.

Leocadia saw and heard nothing.

There was no one else about, as on the previous day, except that, coming back, she beheld Thomas the Warrior in his flower bed.

She spoke to him.

He took no notice.

"The silence is broken," said Leocadia. "You talked to me, at some length."

Thomas paid no attention.

In the summerhouse, Mademoiselle Varc lay sleeping, and Leocadia did not try to wake her.

Returned to her room, Leocadia drew across the white expanse of the prepared wall the guideline of a horizon. Here the snow would end against the silver of the glaciers. And here, below, a penguin would stand, comic and baroque, like one note of music played too loud. She began to sketch it in. It was tall.

Van Orles had not thought to remove the finished canvases, although she might have painted over these. How had he known she would not? Was he clever after all?

She stared at the ship that spilled fruit, and on the sand beside the shells the white thing lay, which now she recognized. It was a snowball.

The hot light made the snow of the wall very rich and

enticing. And in the same way the brown glass showing through the label of the bottle made that snowscape also alluring and warm. Warm as the refrigerator.

White snow gentle as a young summer.

Leocadia drank wine, and let fly a tuft of darkness on the drawn penguin's daggered head.

EIGHT

Paradys

■

But had I wist, before I kissed,
That love had been sae ill to win,
I had locked my heart in a case o' gowd,
And pinned it wi' a siller pin.

Ballard

Everyday about noon, Dr. Volpe toured his kindgom, the lunatic asylum. This gave him a feeling of uneasy and strange power, which he confirmed for himself as the sense of duty. He always hoped that nothing had gone wrong, that none of them had become violent or terribly ill. He liked them to be docile, sitting or wandering about in the straw of the large white rooms. Some nodded or rocked or swatted invisible insects, some sang quietly. These aberrations were normal and he found them almost soothing. The bad smell of confined bodies or those who had messed themselves he was accustomed to. Snuff taking had dulled his nose; he brought with him a scented handkerchief. Now and then there would be an upset. One would not eat, or had set on another, or banged his or her head against a wall. These inmates were restrained, and the sight of their tethers, and the mad-shirts confining their arms, calmed Dr. Volpe.

Sometimes more drastic treatment was required, the Swing or the Waterfall. Doctor Volpe disliked these measures, as he disliked shutting his patients in the upright coffins that permitted only their faces to be seen. He preferred where possible to administer huge doses of opium. As the raving creature sank into oblivion, Dr. Volpe felt an iron clutch slacken on his own muscles.

After his noon perambulation, he would return to his apartment in the adjacent block. Here, when the door was shut, he might, aside from the occasional interruption, have been in some luxurious flat of the City, a gentleman of leisure. There were his shelves of books, his piano, his plants, his various collections—of birds' eggs, butterflies on pins, and so forth. He could potter about all day, and in the evening, the housekeeper brought him his dinner, after which he would drink a bottle of fine brandy.

It was another concern of Dr. Volpe's that some of his warders drank inferior liquor. Although it was, of course, reasonable to drink large amounts of a decent vintage. Amid his brandy Dr. Volpe played scherzos at his piano. His thoughts ranged. Finally he slept well, indeed late into each following day. But to drink all one could afford of a cheap and dreadful gin, which, it was said, was actually poisonous . . . He did not berate the warders. They were curious men and women, bound to their profession by ties Dr. Volpe did not always care to consider. One must not cross them, or one could not exact service. But nevertheless, he had once or twice glimpsed the terrible gin bottles, brown and queerly shaped, with a peculiar label.

Dr. Volpe let out his inner excellence at his piano, and every six months it was carefully tuned.

Playing, he knew a faint loss, for he could have been a great pianist. Misfortune and the pressure of his bourgeoise upbringing had led him where he was.

In fact he did not play very well, fumbling and bluffing works he should not have attempted, firing off like explosions or farts cascades of horrible wrong notes. Besides, and worse, he lacked expression. There was no tenderness, let alone the delicate neurasthenia so often called for. At his most fiery he was at his most appalling. This he did not know.

He was dreamily thinking of his music now as he passed along the galleries above the pens of white rooms.

The women and men were to have been kept separate, but ultimately it was easier to enclose them together. They were scarcely human after all. One woman warder and two men kept watch today, or rather were playing cards at a table.

Dr. Volpe moved over the room like a visiting meteor. All was well. A couple were tethered, the rest moved freely about, or sat in arrested attitudes on the ground. One of the females kissed her hand to the doctor up in the air. He had always liked her gesture, and saluted her gaily. He did not know who she was. Only the troublemakers became, temporarily, known to him.

"Judit is frisky again," said one of the doctor's attendants.

"Judit?"

"The bitch who kissed her hand to you. Better be careful, monsieur doctor."

"Oh, now, now," said Dr. Volpe.

"There is the new female patient," said the woman attendant somberly.

"Ah. Yes."

"She's in the cells."

The "cells" were the place to which newcomers or desperates were assigned. Until their especial malady had been glanced at, they were not herded out with the rest of the prisoners of the asylum.

"Then, I must interview her. Is she lucid?"

"Not very. She's young. About fourteen."

"How tragic," said Dr. Volpe, who was wishing that the cells were unoccupied. He had begun a Russian novel of vast import the night before and longed to get back to it. "What cause is known?"

They shrugged.

"She's crazy. A girl of good family. Suddenly afflicted with *melancholia* and *hysteria*." (The words he would approve of were stressed.) "Her parents were vague."

Dr. Volpe pursed his lips. This kind of mania particularly offended him. Perhaps the woman attendant knew it. Her face was like a wooden box with a nose, and twinkling eyes. She drank the perfidious gin, he knew.

"Well, shall we go along now? I'll see her."

They crossed the last of the gallery and were gone from the rooms. (None of the beings below now seemed aware of them.) They descended stairs and went through a door, and so across a yard where sometimes the mad people were pushed out for exercise. There was a stone block in the middle of the yard. It had been put there for a statue. The statue had been going to represent Madness, with snakes for hair, but in the end this had been thought too strong, and also a waste, for mostly only the mad would see it, and not understand its significance.

The doctor and his warders entered another block, went up a stairway and along other corridors. Below were rooms of treatment, containing the Swing and the Waterfall, and a sample of other apparatus. Above was a set of offices, and near these were the cells.

The wardress unlocked a door. They went in.

Beyond a lattice was a place with a bed, a sort of pallet having one pillow and one blanket. Here someone lay.

Her eyes were open, but they might have been closed. Long bright hair rayed over the pillow. She was dressed in ordinary garments of the City, for she had not yet reached the level of an inhabitant.

"I'll wake her up," said the male warder. His name was Desel. Dr. Volpe believed that he was cruel, but efficient, perhaps necessary.

Desel strolled over, and came into the shut-off portion of the cell. He stood over the bed, and then he slapped the feet of the girl with his stick.

She was still wearing shoes, which had not yet been removed. Nevertheless, the shock boiled through her, and she sat up like a jack-in-the-box. She did not cry out.

"Sleeping Beauty wakes. Doctor's here," said Desel, smiling.

The girl looked at him with utter disbelief. As if he, the warder, were entirely mad.

"Get up, you. Get up and be respectful."

And the girl got off the bed and stood, looking around her, the way a doll would if someone unwisely brought it to life.

"What is your name?" called Dr. Volpe through the lattice. "Do you know?"

"Hilde."

"Good, good. You know your name."

"What is this place?" she asked faintly. "Is it hell?"

"Oh, hell." The doctor laughed. "No, it is to be your heaven."

"I was thrown down. I was held! They struck me," said Hilde. But she seemed bewildered.

"It was for your own good. No doubt you were irrational."

"What is this place?" repeated the girl.

"A hospital. You'll soon be better."

The girl began to cry. This was like a demon coming on her.

A second demon: The warder Desel, started to chuckle with enormous amusement. And the girl, looking up at him, screamed until her throat cracked.

"Go in, comfort her," said Dr. Volpe.

"I? She's dangerous. She tears things," said the woman, Marie Tante.

"Well, then. What do you think?"

"The Waterfall," said Marie Tante. she added mildly, "That will sedate her."

Dr. Volpe grimaced. The Waterfall did not, he had long reasoned, half-kill. It softened, eased.

"She's so young."

"A savage case. Look at that hair. A tricky color. She was vicious with her own mother."

The girl with orange hair had gone on screaming, and they had been forced to shout.

Desel stood by, waiting only for the girl to rush at him. But she did not. She fell suddenly down and lay on the floor. Silence.

"There, the fit's passed."

"Better be sure," said Marie Tante.

"Prepare her," said Dr. Volpe. These people were indispensable. He must follow their advice.

They led Hilde Koster to a large white room that was somehow like a giant's bathtub turned upside down. There was another partition, this time of glass, and beyond it a terrible little black chair, the highchair of a malign child, with bars.

In this chair they put Hilde, Desel and Marie Tante, who, now the girl was to be "subdued" did not seem to fear handling her. The bars of the chair were fastened, across the throat and lap and ankles.

Hilde put out her hands, and Marie Tante slapped them back.

"What are you doing?" Hilde asked.

"Ask no questions," said Marie Tante cheerfully.

"A little wash," said Desel, and grinned.

Hilde seemed embarrassed, confused. All violence had deserted her, run away and left her at their mercy.

The two warders came out of the area with the chair and joined Doctor Volpe behind the glass.

From the ceiling of the room, above the chair, hung a black tube, large and coiled, a sort of serpent.

Dr. Volpe peered through the glass.

"Is she quite ready?"

"Of course. She can't get away."

The doctor stretched out his hand to a lever, then hesitated.

"You shall do it, Desel."

Dr. Volpe had an air of conferring a favor. And Desel was pleased, Marie Tante almost jealous. In fact, Dr. Volpe did not like to perform the action. He would have preferred not to watch.

The warders, though, were avid, and Desel, taking hold of the lever, plunged it down.

In the ceiling the serpent suddenly snapped straight, and out of its headless mouth there rushed an avalanche of water. Its weight was unimaginable, although it had been precisely gauged. It crashed upon Hilde in the little black monster chair and she vanished. Her first shriek of terror was cut off in a frightful choking. Then all audible sound was crushed under the gush of the Waterfall.

Desel's face was now a picture of content, and Marie Tante's was pale with some sort of oblique arousal, pinched and pointing. They stared through the glass, and Dr. Volpe stared too, but with his hand up to his face, shielding his eyes.

For ten minutes the onslaught of the water raged.

"That will be enough," said Dr. Volpe.

"Surely," said Marie Tante, "a few minutes more."

"Oh, yes, then."

"To be sure," said Desel, helping him.

Dr. Volpe thought of his Russian novel. This would soon be over now.

It was over. Marie Tante pushed up the lever, and the incredible Waterfall slackened to a pulse, a flickering tail, a few harsh drops.

The girl sat still in the chair, impossibly not smashed and flushed away. Yet she was colorless, her clothes like rain, her skin like white paper. Even her vibrant hair, though darkened, seemed diluted out.

Marie Tante now managed Hilde alone. She undid the bars of the chair and dragged the drowned creature out of it. Hilde's eyes rolled, yet she was still conscious. Water ran from her mouth. Marie Tante thrust the girl along before her, holding her up by the back of her sodden dress.

Dr. Volpe was more sunny. He shook Desel by the hand before hurrying away to his sanctuary. He had done all he could.

In another cell, Marie Tante and the woman Moule stripped Hilde of her soaked clothing. When she was naked, they prodded at her, saying she was too soft. Marie Tante tweaked Hilde's nipples and asked if she had been a bad girl. "Push your finger in and see," said Moule, but neither she nor Marie Tante did this. The girl, unable to stand, lay on a pallet. They hauled her up. "We should cut her hair." said Moule. Marie Tante scraped back Hilde's wet and deadened tresses and, holding them in her fist, hacked them through with a pair of scissors. Hilde gave a faint cracked cry, the first since the treatment, but she did not seem to realize what had happened, even so. "Shorter," said Moule. "That will do," said Marie Tante. "Look at it," said Moule, "all that hair, at least a meter of it." "It can be sold," said Marie Tante, "but not for much. If it had been black, now. But some ginger cat will buy it in the slums." "Don't forget I helped you cut it," said Moule.

They dressed Hilde, then, in the uniform of her prison. A coarse seamless petticoat and over that the death-white dress of the asylum, tied at the waist with a black cord. On her legs were gartered woolen stockings, and her feet were shoved into heelless cloth shoes.

Hilde was ready now, for the ball.

She was just able to walk, though not to speak, and probably not properly to see or hear.

They conducted her from the building and out across the yard with the stone block. In the shadow away from the sunlight, Moule drew a glinting brown bottle from her pocket. She gulped some liquid down and smacked her lips, then reluctantly passed the gin to Marie Tante.

"They say the vats are all corroded," said Marie Tante. "The rats die that drink the dregs."

"And someone has poured acid in it, too," chortled Moule. "Penguin Gin takes away your pain."

It was almost autumn, and as they crossed the last stretch of yard between the black doors and window-eyed walls of the madhouse, an intimation of fall sweetness drifted from the air—the low sun, the smolder of the trees outside. But the two wardresses did not heed, and the girl was past knowing what it was.

Beyond the asylum, an apron of untended garden ran off into a wood, the trees of which were sometimes cut down. There, over the barricade of an outer wall, lay the countryside, impossible as a foreign land. Even the warders took no notice of it. They too lived in hell, going out rarely, and then in a sort of disdain.

Back inside the first building, Marie Tante and Moule bore Hilde through into the succession of white rooms, where the mad people were.

They moved her out into the middle of the floor, over which the ill-smelling straw extended, giving the space a peculiar farmyard touch. They left her there, like a landmark, and drew back, the two women, to see how the indigenous population received her.

But nothing happened. No one went near.

The mad continued at their insanity quietly, not bothering with the new mad one.

"Here, here," Moule took hold of a man who kneeled on the ground, swaying, "there's a new girl, go and give her a kiss."

The man who swayed began to cry. He curled up on the floor and Moule kicked him with her booted foot.

"Useless," said Marie Tante. "No spirit. Slugs."

One of the male warders had come in, and seeing them, walked up.

"A new lovely for you," said Marie Tante.

"None lovelier than you," said the warder. "Do you have a drink on you?"

"No," said Marie Tante. Moule twitched her pocket uneasily.

Hilde stood alone in the middle of the room. She looked down into the straw, and presently crumpled and slipped over.

"No trouble with her," said the man.

"She's been swimming in the Waterfall."

All around the white forms with cropped or shorn heads bobbed slowly at their antics, like leaves on a pool.

"They make you sick," said the man, "this filth."

They went on into another room, where there were one or two tied up who could sometimes be tormented into noise.

Hilde lay on the straw, and a roach with transparent copper wings crawled over her wrist but did not hurt her.

A woman sat on the straw by Hilde.

Although her hair had been cropped, her head shaved, a dark shadow downed over her skull, which was exquisitely shaped, so that it did not mar her beauty. She was very beautiful, a face of bones and eyes and lips, the thin body of a damask lizard having breasts. Some kind of sphinx?

As Hilde raised her fluttering lids, the woman spoke. "I'm Judit, Queen Judit. I come from a distant country, where I rule. Barges of metal with silk sails go about on my river, and palaces of marble rise. But here I am."

Hilde gazed, her sight returning, into the face of a mother, for the mother to the tiny helpless child is a goddess, infinite and gorgeous, inexorable, yet kind. And all this Judit was. Queen Judit, the mad, who had been a whore in the alleys of Paradys.

"Help me," said helpless Hilde.

"Of course," said Judit. "You mustn't be afraid. This is a great trial. We queens are born to it, and grasp its syntax. But you are only a little angel fallen into the beastliness. Don't be frightened. I'm here."

"Oh," said Hilde.

Judit held her wrist, over which the bracelet of the roach's running had gone. Judit kissed Hilde on the eyebrow.

"Now you're my handmaiden," said Judit. "all will be well."

"But," said Hilde.

"Forget the past, my dear," said Judit. "This is like death. Of course, it will end and we shall go back, in victory. But would you rather come with me to my own country? The mountains embrace the sky. Hawks feed from my hands. I've had a hundred thousand lovers, great kings and lords. Each brought me a fabulous gift, and my house is seventeen stories high."

"How do you reach the top?" asked Hilde, stirring a little, like a wounded bird.

"A flying carpet," said Judit. "How else?"

Pleased, for she had an answer to every question, and liked to display her skill, Judit laughed.

Her teeth were flawless, but for one eyetooth that had been struck from her mouth by a warder (Desel) long ago. She did not recall this. She knew she had lost the tooth in a fight, when she had defended a king who had lain with her, a long dagger in her hand. Judit's beauty had grown with her delusions of beauty, and her strength too. Never, as a starveling harlot, had she had this excellence.

"How did you come here?" asked Hilde.

"A trial. Didn't I say?"

"But why?" Hilde, only half in the world, at once revealed her sense of the truth of Judit, for how should a queen, of Sheba, Egypt, or Andromeda, be *here?*

"There was a face of bronze," said Judit, "which I killed." She was satisfied. "That is why. And how. But I'll triumph over all ruin. One passes every day to whom I blow a kiss. He doesn't know that each kiss is my power; he'll fall under the spell of it."

"Will you help me?" said Hilde, sleepily. The fortitude of Judit had lulled her.

"Poor child. You are mine now. Fear nothing."

And Judit drew Hilde into her lap and held her, stroking the crinkled apricot hair, all that was left of it.

In a hovel Judit had slain a man who had tried to mutilate her for his pleasure. And Judit had gone mad. Mad with anger and justice, to escape the foulness of her world. Now she dwelled among shining thoughts, remembering always she was a queen.

Her fingers were like honey after the horror before. Judit was fire to heal the blows of water. She smelled unclean, but not impure.

The man who had cried had also crept to her, and Judit had not thrust him off. He lay with his mouth against her skirt, asleep.

Judit sang softly of her palaces, of the lions that drank from the river, and the curtains of spun light, and the flowers of her garden, which were fed dead murderers. Her song sounded like gibberish, but this did not matter.

After a time, Hilde told Judit what had happened to her, and Judit listened carefully, her perfect head turned a little to one side. Judit wept, her tears were flames. Hilde saw this, but she was not afraid.

Twice a day, the inmates were fed. In the morning a gruel was brought, and in the evening a type of stew without meat. Both these meals were slops. Bread was served with them that had, as often as not, gone a little moldy.

The cauldrons of food were brought through the rooms on a contraption like a four-legged stretcher with wheels. Certain of the patients were recruited to dole out rations, overseen by the warders with their sticks. To every patient, rounded up and herded to the cauldron, was given a small bowl. There was no cutlery, as even a spoon might be put to dangerous use. They ate with the bread and with their fingers and mouths.

Those who would not eat were watched, and after the third day taken to a room the warders had nicknamed the Banquet Hall. Here a tube was thrust down their throats and they were force-fed on a kind of ant food or sugar water. Sometimes a patient had died from these feasts, from mere shock, or because of the carelessness of the operative, who had inserted the feeding tube into the air vent rather than the esophagus, and so flooded the lungs and drowned them. (These poor patients were always found to have choked while eating too greedily.)

Of such things Judit warned Hilde as she drew her gently to the cauldron.

While they waited their turn, a male warder came to Judit and was familiar with her, putting his hands on her buttocks. Judit laughed in his face. Her body had no scruples and no modesty, and she was, besides, a queen. But when the warder turned to Hilde, as if to extend the treatment to her, Judit came between them, smiling. "Get off, you old whore," said the warder, and backed away, menacing Judit with his stick.

In the bottom of the cauldron, under the soggy vegetables, something glittered.

"There are spikes there," said Judit.

Once a small man, a dwarf, had hidden in the tureen and so got to the kitchens, where he took a knife and attacked some of the warders. Now the spikes were in the pot to prevent another such attempt.

Hilde did not want to eat, but Judit urged her to take a little, especially the disgusting bread. The warders had not realized, it seemed, that the fungus on the bread helped keep off infections. Judit's grandmother in the alleys had taught her this, but she had forgotten, and now explained a great physician had exposed the fact to her.

After the cauldron was removed, most of the warders went off to their own dinner of meat and potatoes in another building. Only four were left on duty, two playing cards in a central room and two patrolling.

"What is it they drink?" asked Hilde.

"A venom," said Judit. "I, too, have tasted it. Unlike the wines of my own country."

Judit took Hilde by the hand through the many large mirror-like white rooms, on which now late afternoon was gathering from the high barred windows that showed nothing but the closing sky.

Hilde stared at the mad people in still wonder. She was so shocked, so wrecked, that now her capacity for fear was virtually gone. She had entered a translucent state, as human things sometimes do when they lose their personalities. Everything that had happened to her seemed to have happened to another. All the world was alien and illogical and this piece of it no more so than the rest. She wanted nothing, except perhaps eventually to sleep. She was glad of Judit's company and seemed to have known her countless years.

Several of the mad acknowledged Judit, and some even bowed or curtseyed to her. But others were too busy. One was an insect and waited in her web for flies and another was talking to spirits or invisible people. One crawled in a circle around and around.

In perhaps the third room a man had been tied to the wall by a thong about his throat. He wept ceaselessly and his neck was raw from trying to pull free. Judit went to him and wiped up his tears with her long hair, which no more existed. A second man was in a mad-shirt, and he rolled along the floor, biting at the straw and making strange hoarse barks. The warders had beaten his legs on their patrol.

In a fifth room there was an arrangement of old broken furniture that rose in a hill higher than the gallery that ran along the wall. The hill was some distance from this, and from all the windows. At its top sat a skinny man, looking out like a gull from a roof.

"There's Maque," said Judit.

She began to climb the structure, her firm legs, bare of stockings, revealed up to the white knees. Hilde did not follow, for though she was no longer able to be afraid, some physical nervousness remained. But then Judit turned and beckoned her, and Hilde did go up the stair of furniture, which was actually quite solid, its uneven places simple to avoid.

Aloft, on a table, sat Maque, and here they joined him.

The glory of the height was its view through a window. Although about six meters away, unreachable, it showed sections of burning sky and the crowns of burning trees. The sun was setting there, as if it had never before done so, and meant to make the world pay attention.

They stared at it, their faces lit like potter's clay.

Maque was extraordinarily thin, and in his ears were tears from which the rings had been torn years ago, on his arrival at the asylum. Elsewhere now, in the City, his ill-omened earrings were worn; they had got free.

"I've sailed the sea," said Maque presently. "I had a pet monkey that died of old age when he was twenty-three. I've seen Eastern ports where women dance naked but their faces are veiled in black. I've smoked hemp under the shelter of an elephant and eaten powdered pearl for the pox, which cured me." His conversation, or rather monologue, was somewhat like Judit's. He said, "Ten men gone overboard in a tempest. We came to an island. There were unicorns there, but our mate said they were only a kind of goat. A virgin may capture a unicorn."

The sun went under the window, and the bars stood on

thick burnished sky. Shadows spread among them. Below the hill of furniture some of the mad people made small sounds.

"This child can never," said Judit, "capture a unicorn. She's been violated."

Hilde was not shamed. She nodded, distantly.

"Yes," she said, as of another, "that happened to me."

"She went to him in love," said Judit.

"Look," said Maque. And he got up on one knee and pulled from under his right thigh a brown glass bottle. "Empty, of course," he said, "Thrown away near the latrine."

"A gin bottle," said Judit. She took it and gave it to Hilde. Hilde had never seen such a thing. On the label was a great black and white bird with a flush of amber next to its head. Behind was whiteness.

"I never saw a land such as that," said Maque the sailor. "A cold country with mountains of snow. But I heard of them. The freeze forms vast cliffs of ice that float into the sea, and when they meet they clash like glass. These birds live there. Penguins, they're called. They can't fly, but stalk about like kings."

"Are they little birds?" asked Hilde childishly, for this was her protection now, between Judit and Maque.

"Some, maybe," said Maque. He pointed at the bottle. "But not this fellow. Look at him. He could be seven feet high. And his beak's a knife."

Below the furniture, many of the inmates had gathered close, and looked up at Maque. Maque rose, and taking back the bottle, he raised it. One last spark of sunlight came in at its top and shot a ray from sky to ground.

"And they said," said Maque, "the snow is warm, there. So warm you can lie down and sleep in it like a feather bed. And flowers grow when the sun shines on the ice. The sun never sets but hangs low, so it's always dawn or sunset. That is Penguin Land."

"I'd do without my country, to see that," said Judit.

"But," said Hilde, some dim rationality struggling deep within her. Yet she had no use for it any more, and abruptly let it go. "You could play at snowballs in Penguin Land," she said, "and never burn your hands on the snow."

"You would never be hungry or thirsty," said Judit. "Fruit and sweets grow on the trees and wine runs down the ice."

The light ray melted from the bottle and went out.

The room was very dark.

And through the doorway stamped three wardresses, jingling their keys.

"Get down, you bitches," shouted one at Judit and Hilde.

"What is it now?" asked Hilde.

"Now they lock us into our dormitories," said Judit. She smiled, "After dark, we're sinful, so they must separate the women from the men."

When they were near the bottom of the furniture, Marie Tante seized Hilde and pulled her off, bruising her. "Not quiet yet? Perhaps you'll need more subduing."

The women were marched away by women, and men came in a crowd, toting their sticks, to get charge of the male inmates.

Darkness was full now in the asylum. One of the female warders carried a lamp, and the outer corridors had been sparsely lighted.

They passed up a stair, and a door was unlocked. Into the women's dormitory they went.

The beds lay along the floor. They were straw pallets covered by thin blankets and having each a soiled and impoverished pillow. Every place was foul, and a worse smell came from buckets of necessity set at intervals and doubtless not frequently emptied. On a wall facing the beds and buckets was a wooden cross. This was ignored by one and all.

The women went where they wished, or where they felt they must, and sat or lay down.

Marie Tante drove Hilde the length of the room to a pallet apparently unclaimed.

"Here, my lady. Your couch."

Hilde got onto the bed and crouched there. After all,

fear remained of this woman who seemed grown to a pre-
posterous size. (Why not then a giant penguin?)

"You'll have lice by tomorrow," said Marie Tante."What
a stink in here. We must hose these beasts down."

"That one's been wetted already," said Moule.

The third wardress giggled and swung up her lamp, to
make the room career and spin. The madwomen gazed at
this phenomenon silently.

The wardresses left them, locking the door.

The room was black, and in the black the women rustled
and whispered. One moaned over and over.

Hilde sat in dull dismay, for Judit was far off. The
awful smell oppressed her, but then she sensed a current
of cleaner air. Some tiny panes of glass were missing
from the window above, and now a night breeze blew. It
would be cold in winter, not warm as the snows of the
Penguin Land.

An hour later, the moon entered the window. And so the
room.

On the space of black floor below the powerless crucifix,
the milk-white squares of the barred window appeared.

One by one, two by two, the madwomen left their ver-
minous beds and came down to the pool of light.

Here they moonbathed. Some washed in the moonlight,
rubbing their arms and faces, or lifting up the whiteness
between their legs. Others lay down and swam among the
squares. The woman who moaned tried to prize the shadow
bars away and could not, and crept back, made dumb, to her
bed.

Judit stood up in the center of the reflection, her face
raised into the light, which tinted her like snow.

But the moon passed over, and total darkness returned.
And in this dark, the door was unlocked, not brashly now,
but with stealth.

The male warder who had come after the moon sought
Judit the whore among the women, and mounted her. They
heard her say, in a voice of velvet, "What, are you here again,
oh my king? What an honor." And then they heard the man

131

strike her. It was Tiraud, who would drink to capacity and then seek out the queen of harlots. Soon finished. He called her filthy names and exclaimed now over the fetor of the dormitory.

At the door another chuckled. And away along the corridors there started a wild whooping and screaming.

Hilde sprang up, and Judit was by her, for even so soon she knew Judit's touch.

"They do things to the men they don't dare try with us."

The awful crying went on, and the women huddled off their beds. They congregated around Judit, as they had gone to the moon pool. Her skirt was sticky, but she was yet a queen.

When the cries stopped, there came instead a crazy clatter in the air, and at the door the jailers laughed raucously.

Something flew against Hilde, leather and fur, and she shrieked in turn. No, fear was not all gone.

All about, the women gurned in panic. Into the dark it was not possible truly to see, only to hear, as they burrowed and howled and ran at the walls. The other thing also did that, swooping from side to side.

Judit had stood up again, and she raised her arm, and mysteriously she was half visible as if faintly luminous from within.

So, by Judit's shine, Hilde saw the bat the warders had let go in the room. It whirled overhead and dipped suddenly down, settling on Judit's fingers as the hawks did in her dream country.

A demon with a fairy face, the bat folded its wings.

Judit carried it to the wall, and put it there, and the bat detached itself and crawled upward, into the high embrasure of the window. Here it found a broken pane and slipped through.

"Very good, very good," said the men at the door. "She's clever, is Judit."

As they locked the door behind them, the cries began again across the building. Dr. Volpe, two blocks away in brandy sleep, would not hear them. And if he did? Lunatics were noisy.

Hilde lay back. She pushed the crying from her and thought of the bat in the cool sky, and of the warm snow.

The mandarin leaves fell slowly and sparingly from the trees on the lawn and in the wood. Gray geese passed over.

An extravagant hothouse built for Dr. Volpe on the lawn outside the asylum blocks began to burgeon with harvest, black grapes on a vine, apricots, toasted roses.

The mad people were never allowed as far as the lawn, and never beheld it from the windows.

There had been plans for a summerhouse too, maybe a small lake. But these things had never come to be.

One evening an agent brought Dr. Volpe a wonderful new prisoner, a dead butterfly with huge bright wings.

Hilde did not cause any trouble, and Marie Tante had lost interest in her. One of the men had taken to shrieking, and was conducted to the Swing, where, in a sort of box, they rotated and reeled him until he vomited and swooned. Thereafter he sat quietly in his mad-shirt on the straw.

Hilde came to recognize her fellows, though usually not by any name.

Judit showed her the poet Citalbo, who had gone insane from reading drama and writing verses. Citalbo walked solemnly from room to room, sometimes scribbling on small pieces of paper that the warders allowed him, as Dr. Volpe had decreed. The warders often stole the papers, however. This did not appear to matter. What Citalbo wrote now was nonsense, frequently illegible. He never seemed to miss his former works, or anything that was stolen, as if, once he had put down an idea, God had it in safekeeping.

During the days of straw, Judit occasionally told stories, histories perhaps, of her queendom. At night also, now and then, for they would not always sleep at night in the dormitory, as by day sometimes they would. Maque sat upon his hill. They did not speak or approach him again. The brown bottle had vanished—confiscated? No one mentioned the Penguin Land.

One morning the warders beat a man in front of all the others. He had been running to and fro and the warders caught him suddenly and threw him down, kicking him with their boots and striking him with their sticks. The noise rose in the madhouse then like a storm in a cage of parakeets. The screams and cries of the mad did not quite overcome the oaths and grunts of the male warders or the shrill giggles of the three wardresses who were present.

The beaten man was left lying, and somehow recovered, or at least did not die.

When Dr. Volpe went along the galleries at noon, the lunatics were generally very still. Some tried to hold their breath. Most did not know who Dr. Volpe was, only that he appeared rather like a clockwork toy, at a certain time, also that he presided over the worst tortures.

There were other incidents: The shaving of a woman's head, the force-feeding of another, a drunken song the warders indulged in without warning. The afternoon that something was added to the slops which gave the inmates pains in their bellies, and how Judit raved about the healing tinctures of her land, and between calmly told Hilde this had occurred before, and would soon pass. By night, intermittently, Tiraud, or others, came into the women's dormitory, to use Judit's body. She did not resist these rapes. Once or twice some other woman was violated as well or instead. In particular darknesses, outcry resounded from the men's cloister.

The moon came often to the women's barred window, at different hours, and laid its light along the floor. The women did not always go down to it. And one night Hilde stood alone in the midst of the pool, staring up at the window, its source, above. She had lost all comprehension of the place she was in, she did not look for rescue, if she ever had. The image of Johanos Martin had long since withered from her, as had her night game, the sweet masturbation of her innocence. In a manner, the asylum had done what it had promised, driving out the devils that had brought her here, but only to replace them with others.

Judit, who had been preyed on three times that night, lay sleeping. Hilde went to her and curled up by Judit's feet. It was cold. Hilde thought of the Penguin Land.

Dr. Volpe dusted the leaves of a palm, and standing back, surveyed its effect against the autumnal window. He could see down toward the hothouse, and the chestnuts and oaks of the wood. This was a pleasing view and might be that of any country retreat.

A knock on the outer door alerted him and he pulled a child's sulky face.

His housekeeper entered.

"The gentleman from the theater, Dr. Volpe."

Dr. Volpe had forgotten.

His face of distaste became harder and more adult.

"Very well, you may send him in."

Dr. Volpe paused beside the case with the new butterfly in it. He would linger just long enough to show the visitor what was important, and proper.

But the visitor, the blustering gentleman from the Goddess of Tragedy, launched at once into a speech, not waiting to be asked.

"We are delighted that you'll do as we desired, Dr. Volpe. This will render my actors a great service. And in the course of art—"

"It is a disgrace," said Volpe, his face swollen now. "To bring sightseers here. As if into a zoological garden. These people are my patients."

"Quite, quite." The visitor brushed Volpe's words and stance aside. "But as you're aware, the minister has overridden your objection. I'm sure you don't set yourself above him, doctor."

Volpe was ruffled. He was at the mercy of upperlings and underlings.

"If he thinks so. I'm not certain the minister was correctly informed."

"Oh, *quite* correctly."

"To have your troupe here, staring at these poor deranged souls."

"What harm can it do?" said the agent from the theater. "And so much good. The lunatics won't notice, I expect. And for my actors, an invaluable help in the preparation of the mad scene for our next production."

"I dissociate myself from the proceeding," said Dr. Volpe.

"Of course. I suppose your warders are capable of overseeing the affair."

Dr. Volpe imagined his warders poking the mad people with sticks, forcing them to caper and wail to interest the actors. But they would do it, too, if he was present, and then there would be the shame of it. The warders would expect to receive large tips.

He did not offer the agent refreshment, and when he was gone, Dr. Volpe walked among his birds' eggs, caressing their smoothness (each a tiny coffin, but he did not consider that.)

Soon after dawn, the dormitory was unlocked and the women were hustled out again, down to the common rooms. Today it was not the same.

Marie Tante, and the wardress Bettile, stood at the doorway. They took hold of Judit at once. "This one," they said, "she's much admired."

The other women, thinking Judit had been singled out for some therapy (punishment), shied away, all but Hilde.

Marie Tante reached and gripped Hilde's arm.

"This is a pretty one. Look how quickly her hair's grown back. You'll have to be shorn again, my lady."

Hilde hung speechless in her grasp. But now Bettile grabbed two other girls from among the women.

"These will do. For the *pretty* ones."

"Hah! They'll pass."

The four chosen women and the one other Bettile hauled out, who whimpered and then sobbed, they led away along the corridor to a big tiled area.

Hilde felt again the invasion of terror. This was like the white room in which she had been tortured. She could recall very little of it, but she had thought that she died there, and came back very changed.

"Don't be afraid," Judit said sternly.

The warders told them to take off their garments. Judit removed hers almost blithely. Despite her captivity, she was still very beautiful, and though her breasts were not those of a girl, they were full as two blown roses.

Marie Tante jeered at Judit: "Not bad for an old whore."

But Judit laughed, and Marie Tante turned her attention to the other women.

These were malformed and undernourished, or oddly fatty, their bodies blemished by moles and pimples, inner subsidences of the flesh.

Hilde was ashamed to bare herself, and Bettile charged at her and ripped the clothes off her body.

"Too proud, eh? What have you got to be proud of, ugly little runt?"

When all the women were naked, hoses were turned on them. The water was icy cold but not extremely violent. Some fell down. Hilde dropped to her knees. Yet, since the water only occasionally covered her head, it did not completely recall the former horror. Almost, she missed the landmark of it.

When the sluicing was over, rough sheets were flung to the women, and those that could dried themselves. Two could not, and these Marie Tante saw to with harsh buffeting swipes.

They were given new tunics, and white sashes, bundled into them.

The warders mocked the women. "Just need a spot of powder." "Some flowers for the hair."

They were removed next to a narrow chamber, and awarded some of the breakfast gruel. One of the women spilled the fluid on her new robe, and Bettile cuffed her. "Dirty sow. Do you think you'll get another washing? You'll have to go as you are."

"What will they do to us?" Hilde whispered.

Judit said, "Sometimes ladies and gentlemen pay to look at us."

Hilde relapsed in apathy, but when they were presently taken out again, she stayed close to Judit.

The women were then put into a long room that faced onto the yard with the stone block, and here they were left some hours, with Bettile to watch them, but Bettile drank her gin, set out her cards, and fell asleep.

Two of the women sat down on the floor, where one wept until the snores of Bettile, perhaps taken for a reprimand and threat, silenced her. Judit and Hilde and the fifth woman went each to one of the three windows that looked onto the courtyard. There they stood in a row.

Outside it was a fine, still fall day, the misty sunshine soft as gauze. At the center of the court, about the stone, was a curious structure, in fact a makeshift stage Tiraud and some of the warders had put up. It was only a foot or so high, and composed of trestles, over which some sheeting had been draped.

On the far side of the court was something even more incongruous. An awning had been erected and armchairs put under it. And there was a table with a white cloth on which now began to be laid plates of food under napkins, dishes of fruit from the hothouse, coppery pomegranates, oranges and apricots, and black grapes. Into buckets went slabs of ice. Judit said, "That will be for the champagne. Someone has looked after them. Perhaps they're princes," and she spat abruptly on the floor.

"Ice from Penguin Land," said Hilde, to please her.

"No," said Judit, "the ice from there would never melt. The ice there is warm."

And Hilde was humbled by her mistake. She put her hand on the warm glass of the window.

Her back had begun to ache from standing immobile so long. But the draw of the courtyard, a view it was possible to gaze at, kept her there. Besides, she waited nervously to see who had come. She had forgotten people—she and the inmates of the asylum were not people—and so in turn human things from the outer world had become like wild beasts. What would they do, or require? Would they sniff and paw, or rend? She dreaded that she would have to show herself to them, but not because of the state to which she had been reduced, only because they were so alien.

Now she said, to please Judit again, for Judit was real, "What is the name of the Penguin Land?"

"Maque will know," said Judit. She added, "They'll display Maque. He's a model patient, controlled and articulate. And Citalbo, perhaps. Because he speaks poetry."

There were sounds below. One of the black doors opened, and Desel came forth. He was taking on the role of guide that Dr. Volpe might have assumed, and Desel had dressed up in suit of clothes and a high collar. He looked fearsome and terrible, like some species of poisonous insect that has adopted the gaudy wings of something it has recently killed. The fifth woman at the window groaned, and going sadly away, sat down on the floor with the other two.

Out of the doorway after Desel came the beasts who were people, the beasts who had come to visit the zoo.

There were a couple of ladies in flowered dresses, with hats and parasols, and a group of men, two rather tall, each smartly dressed.

Hilde drew back from the window.

Hilde pointed.

Her fingertip touched the glass. Now it was cold.

And Bettile awoke.

"Oh, are the bastards here? I expect Desel will give you bitches autumn crocuses to hand to those fine, jumped-up ladies, to show how well we've trained you."

Judit turned her shaven head on her white neck, like a snake, looking at Hilde, then turned back and looked down again into the yard.

Hilde moved even farther back, her arm still outstretched, as if frozen.

"What's up?" said Bettile. She rose, taking as she did so a swig of gin.

139

"Johanos Martin," said Hilde. Her face suffused with an appalling embarrassment.

"Oh, the great Martin," said Bettile. "Fancy, you know the name. When were you at the theater?" She elbowed Hilde's shrinking body aside and peered out. "Well, so that's the bugger. The tallest one, I've heard he's tall."

The gray eyes of Johanos Martin passed smoothly over the windows, seeing nothing. He was accustomed to looking up, from a stage, blind to those who hung above.

Hilde ran into a corner and curled herself together. Bettile swung round and marched toward her.

"Get up, slut. Get up, I say."

She pulled Hilde to her feet and Hilde screamed. She forgot who Bettile was, and fought with her, and Bettile felled Hilde with a single blow.

In the gilded day, ten lunatics were let out on the platform.

In the awning shade, drinking freely the wine their theater had sent them, picking at segments of chicken and orange, the actors watched. It made a change for them, someone else putting on a show. They did not completely like it, you could see. And they stared acutely to tell how much better they would be able to do it, to act the insane.

Desel did not have his stick now but a cheap florid cane he had bought in the City. With this he poked at the madmen, making them whine or snort or shy. Sometimes they did not respond at all. Some crawled, others walked in a curious apelike way. The more interesting specimens were directed to the front of the trestles.

The ladies made disapproving sounds over the one who drooled from his permanently grinning, tooth-barricaded mouth. His smile was a rictus that never went away, his lips dark and his teeth long and sallow. His eyes were thick with pain he no longer considered.

"The man who grins," said Desel, as if he had invented all ten lunatics, carefully, in a laboratory. "He never speaks, and forces food between his fangs only when we make him.

His grin goes on while he sleeps. What a happy sight to keep before you. Imagine this one in your sitting room." He was a touch impertinent, Desel, for now he was dressed up as gentleman, and they were only actors.

After the grinning man, a man came who seemed to think he was a dog. He moved on all fours, panting, and now and then he licked his own hands.

And after this one came the one on a tether, led by Tiraud. When Tiraud jabbed the tethered man with his stick, the madman began to sing in a shrill voice songs that were just recognizable as old ballads of love.

Presently they drove forward the man who was sur-rounded by a swarm of invisible wasps, at which he beat wildly. Tiraud struck this man's ankle, and the man fell upon it, biting and snapping at his own flesh, trying to pull something not there away from him.

Others were left standing in the backgound, where they drooped or padded about in small circles.

After these first men, some women were brought, shaven-headed and in matted gowns. The wardresses, nota-bly Marie Tante, shouted at them, and the women moved about with a hobbled gait, like lost cows that do not under-stand but know the smiting of sticks.

Desel stepped into the middle of the stage. He com-menced giving a lecture on the types and attributes of madness. He sensed the actors had become bored and saw that they grew restless. He did not like them. Nobodies risen to fame by dint of luck, and whoring. Look at the actresses—strumpets. And the men, doubtless lax of morals, perhaps given to unnatural vices.

The tallest man, the one called Martin, looked at Desel with icy and expressionless eyes. These eyes flustered Desel. He wished for a moment Martin had been in his power.

But it was the other man, Roche, who called out, "Ah, come on, come on."

Desel concluded his address hurriedly. Turning, he struck one of his charges so the man squeaked and leapt over the stage, making the trestles creak ominously.

The crowd of male and female lunatics was herded aside, and some, the most troublesome, were removed from the court. (A couple had soiled themselves from fear or need.)

Now the women came who were supposed attractive, and fairly docile. Desel had thought the ginger girl, Hilde, would be among them, but she was missing.

Bettile led the women forward.

"Curtsey to the gentlemen and ladies," said Bettile, and swung her rod at the backs of legs. Two women curtsied, and one tumbled to her knees. Judit stood. "This one won't," said Bettile. "Tell the people why you won't."

Judit glanced at Bettile, then she gazed at Roche. Her dark eyes passed through him, and Judit murmured, audible and sorrowfully, "A queen does not obeise herself."

Roche stood up and doffed his hat. He bowed.

His eyes were not at all full of mockery. He said, "I believe she is."

But Judit only smiled forgivingly, and raised her eyes to the sky above the buildings.

Soon three or four more men were brought to be shown off. Among them was Maque.

"This man was a sailor," said Tiraud. "It was the sea sent him crazy. Now he invents lands that don't exist."

"All lands exist," said Maque.

"How true," said Roche. "In the world and out of it."

Roche was drunk perhaps. Most of the champagne bottles were empty. The actresses were flushed. Even Martin had a slight trace of color in his face.

"Tell the gentlemen about your travels, Maque," said Tiraud.

Maque said, "My last voyage was to this place. Here they tore the metal rings out of my ears. I was locked in a room no bigger than a hutch, and later in an upright box. I could not move my hands. I was fed on rotted bread and stale water."

"He attacked a warder," Desel explained carefully.

Tiraud said grimly, "Speak of your sea trips, sailor."

Maque closed one eye. "I forget."

"The Swing for you," whispered Tiraud in Maque's mutilated ear.

Maque said, "I saw a land once, covered with snow. And on the trees grew bottles of gin."

Tiraud hit Maque across the spine.

Maque did not turn. He stared away, as Judit had done.

All the champagne was gone; the actors had become instead the receptacles.

And the warders were full of spirits.

They brought Citalbo, the poet who had gone mad.

He stood on the stage, and spoke to Johanos Martin in a sonorous voice of leaden silver.

"Why," said Roche, startled, "he's saying your lines from the play—the Roman—"

"He speaks very well," said Martin, and gazed up the short distance at Citalbo.

"Empires shall go down like suns," Citalbo said. "And ships beach in the bays as locusts do, on the firm corn."

He inclined his head, and waited courteously.

Johanos Martin laughed. He got up, and said, ringingly and perfectly, "So it was, and so it shall be always," and paused like a coquette.

And Citalbo went on: "Until the earth is a dry husk and the sky falls, and in never any house—"

"A girl sits," Martin said, "to braid her hair. Or a warrior stands—"

"To buckle on the brass of war. But then," Citalbo said, "we shall be dust, and thus—"

"Who cares for those that do not think of us?" Martin finished.

Roche applauded. The other actors and actresses were caught up, and put their gloved and bead-garlanded paws together.

"Monsieur," said Martin, for Citalbo had dared to speak his lines with great beauty and skill, "as I am, you are: an actor."

"Then you, sir," replied Citalbo, softly, carryingly, "must be as I am. Mad."

Martin's face closed. His eyes were steel. He drained his glass, and turned away as Maque and the others had not been able to.

"Let's leave. We've seen enough."

"Oh," said one of the actresses, with whom once Martin had made unsatisfactory love, "his lordship is suddenly squeamish."

"Not at all. I consider you. The sun can be harsh on the complexion at your age, Susine."

Dismayed, Dr. Volpe had stepped about his room. His books gleamed and he read their titles, remembering *I have this, and this.* He examined eggs and ornaments (*and this*). Across the blocks of the asylum things went on, but he might pretend they did not. This was his apartment, his country retreat. The palm in the window, the autumn woods.

He went to the case where the new butterfly was displayed, and stopped—in revulsion, distress.

The pinned specimen, which had been like flame and night, was crumbling. Its wings were showering off in soot and embers. Its body had twisted as if tortured, into a corkscrew.

When they brought Hilde from the tiny box where they had locked her, the "coffin," her head was shaven like a bronze ball. She was shut now into a straitjacket, a mad-shirt, her arms secured across her body. One of her shoes had been subtracted.

They put her in the straw. She could barely move.

The women came.

As animals softly nose at each other in the winter fields, just so they approached, not actually touching, but mute, reserved, at one. They knew her. She was themselves.

And then Judit was there, and sat by Hilde.

Judit spoke of the land of snow, where the lovely fruit grew and the dawn-and-sunset sun poured out its jasper radiance. Birds sang and far off the sea glistened, waters that were not cold and into which the wine streams cascaded.

144

Hilde listened.

When Judit ceased, she said, "Judit, I'm dying."

"No, poor child. You must simply endure."

"But I am. You see, my blood's turned to water."

Judit stroked Hilde's face. "Why do you think so?"

"Because my time hasn't come. Not for weeks."

"Your time? Oh. The female cycle . . . Once, I too." Judit frowned. "My womb's burned out. Yours also? Be thankful. They shame us here, when we bleed."

Hilde bowed her head. "Then this is good?"

"Oh, yes," said Judit strongly. "Be glad, dear."

NINE

Paradise

Love that moves the sun and the other stars.

Dante Alighieri

Months had passed, but Paradise had no seasons, as it had no sun, no moon.

They had killed with cords, but then came poisons. This often called for a particularly intimate attack—besides, they tried to find new types of bane. It taxed their ingenuity, and this time Felion and Smara put off the task. They did not poison anyone. They told each other, when they met, of their oppression at shirking the labor. Both had come close to it. Smara had even lured a man to her apartment, meaning to put some of the acid from the clockwork cat's leaking panel into a glass of wine. But then she had not done it. The man had left resentfully; obviously he had expected something. "He may only have anticipated sex," Felion told her.

They did not talk about the labyrinth, or the City beyond.

The mystery was like an ache that never went away.

Smara dreamed that she was moving through a pale warm building. An elderly woman in white was hurrying down a corridor, and when she passed Smara, the woman said, "Go away, Lucie. Go to your nurse."

There was a long room that gave on a flagged patio, and here some men sat at ease, drinking tea. They did not seem to see Smara, who prowled about them, half wondering if she might drop poison in their cups. One man smoked a pipe and another toyed with an eye glass. They were elegant, and one very handsome, with longish silken hair. Smara took a fruit or vegetable from a bowl on a table. She threw it past them, out onto the lawn. There it rolled like an orange snowball, away and away, until it hit a low fence in the distance.

Smara did not tell Felion about this dream, in which there had been clarity, daylight, and no mist.

Felion did not dream about the other City, or its environs.

They walked the broad fogbound boulevards, that sometimes echoed at their voices or rang with unknown laughter.

One afternoon, they came, seemingly by chance, to the foot of the hundred steps.

They stood for some time, as if awaiting another person.

Then, in fits and starts, frequently stopping to stare away across the blank of Paradise (the cathedral tower was invisible today), they climbed the steps.

On the Bird Terrace they did not pause. Felion opened the door with the chant of numbers. They went into the house, through, and down.

In the basement a small machine had woken and was bustling about, moving little metal boxes, cogs, and bunches or wire from one place to another, apparently without logic.

As they walked along the track, it skittered after them, then veered away, twittering angrily.

"It believes we're intruders," he said.

"Are we?"

"Yes, but we were meant to be."

Then the ice wall was ahead of them.

Felion picked up the torch he had left lying, and lit it.

"We can run through," he said. "Keep hold of my hand or we may be separated again."

"I'm not afraid," she said. "And that seems wrong."

"They've done something to the door of the artist's house," he said. "That may make it difficult to leave the premises. We must break through *outside* the house. You must *will* that, too."

"I don't know how."

"Demand it then, aloud, of the labyrinth. How else did you get in and out before?"

"It seemed . . . easy," she said.

"It is easy. Yes," he added, "of course, it must all be wrong. The heat of the torch will finally spoil the ice—what then? We have to decide, Smara, where we want to be."

In the labyrinth they did not run, but walked briskly, she striding and he slightly checking his pace, to stay in step with each other.

A glowing thing bloomed in the wall.

"Look!" she said.

He saw it too, presumably the same vision. A child watching a tiger in a cage. It was a horrible child, sneering at the incredible and flawless animal, which, if the bars had not been there, would have destroyed the child fastidiously and at once.

Then the image dispersed.

They had come suddenly into the oval heart of the labyrinth.

On the floor was a fruit, an orange fruit.

Felion let go of Smara's hand, bent down, and picked the fruit up. But Smara was gazing at the bird-headed thing that had risen above out of the ice. If anything it was now more clear, more like the statues on her uncle's terrace.

Felion tossed the orange fruit up at the ice statue. The fruit struck it a weightless blow and sailed on, and over into nothing, whence, surely, it had come.

"I'm not afraid of that now, either," said Smara."It's only a shape."

Felion took her by her hand again quickly.

"Let's go on."

A sound rose, the oceanic breathing roar of the labyrinth.

Smara moved reluctantly. "I thought it would crumble a little, when I said it didn't frighten me."

Beyond the heart, keeping to the left, they strode forward.

"Remember," he said, "the *outside* of the woman's house. The street there."

149

"Are you still holding my hand?" she asked.

Felion hesitated, and as he did so, the torch flickered as if a wind rushed through the maze. And Smara slid away from him.

It was as though she were moved away on runners. She did not seem to notice. When he called out in alarm, she only nodded. *"Outside* the house," she repeated.

And then she was furled aside into the ice wall.

Perhaps Felion had been pulled aside in this way as he followed his uncle, or the man who resembled his uncle, those months before when he had come back here alone.

Felion was appalled nevertheless. He tried to approach the wall, but it was solid, ungiving, and Smara had gone.

He had no choice, it seemed to him, but to proceed to the labyrinth's extremity. Maybe, anyway, he would find her there.

When he reached the end of the tunnels, the torch was fluttering sickly. Ahead, in the opening, lay a cloudy void.

Felion spoke aloud to it, telling it harshly what he expected it to become, the street outside the artist's house. But even when he walked right up to it, the exit from the labyrinth showed nothing but formless clouds, save far away, he seemed to glimpse a shape like a mountain.

"But it's easy," he said. He dropped the torch by the exit point, and plunged his hand and arm out into the cloudy aberration.

Perhaps the tiger's cage was there, and his hand had gone in through the bars.

Felion drew his arm back. It was whole.

Then he shut his eyes, lowered his blond head, and jumped through the gap straight into the cloud.

Smara stood on the golden bank of a malt-dark river. She was not distressed. She had not been so before, when she had lost Felion and arrived in another world. Not to be distressed was possibly distressing.

And this was not the other City. Assuredly not.

The air had an exceptional brightness and lucidity. Distant mountains embraced the sky.

Below, on the honey strand, tigers and lions were feeding on something among the onyx boulders.

Above, a city did line the bank. High, white, pillared buildings, glistening with metal. Huge trees which might have been palms, but their fronds curved to the ground.

Around Smara was a garden, and everywhere in it girls in white were watering the flowers. Probably Smara had not been noticed for this reason, for in her hand was a bronze dipper filled by water. Smara went quietly up the slope of the turf and came out on a walk. On the horizon was a marble palace of extreme tallness. Nearby, a queen or empress was seated under a white sunshade. She was beautiful, more beautiful even than Smara's mother. Around her throat was a rope made of twenty or so chains of enormous pearls. Her black hair fell from a starry coronet to her feet.

A man sat at her feet.

He was tanned almost to leather, and in his ears winked diamonds. He was telling the beautiful queen boldly about a voyage he had made in a timber ship. He showed her on a map that was stretched over the grass.

"But she ran aground, Majesty. We lost the strange fruit and the priceless glass vessels. I was there ten days, with my men, before the king of the land heard what had befallen us and sent his chariots to our assistance."

"I have never known luck like yours," said the queen. "Maque, you know you're worth more to me than any cargo. But who," she added, "is that girl, listening?"

"Your favorite handmaiden, surely."

"No, she has hair like ginger spice. This one has hair like cream. Who are you, young girl?"

"Smara," Smara said, and she bowed. But then the dipper spilled all over her skirt.

"She's in search of some other country," said the queen. "Be careful," she added, "not all of them are good."

"Madame," said the sailor, who had been called Maque, "in a way, it's true of us all—that we search for other countries. Of the mind, the heart, and the soul. And sometimes even we search for hell on earth."

The queen smiled. She laid her hand on his arm. "Where are you going?" the queen asked Smara.

"To Felion, my brother."

"Do you love him?" asked the queen.

"Yes."

"Love can do anything," said the queen.

Smara turned, and a cloud was there behind her. She dropped the dipper on the grass, and then—

And then it seemed she was her mother, falling, falling from the whirling tower, into the stony mist.

The sun was beginning to set, and for a while he forgot even his sister.

Felion was high up, above the City, the wonderful City that had not been corrupted by mist. He could see all of it. The scales of its million roofs, like plates of a crocodile's back, its towers and domes, and far off the loops of its river, tiger's-eye, catching the rays of the extraordinary sun.

But then he wanted her to see this, this fabulous City, beautiful beyond any dream or wish. Oh, he wanted Smara to be here with him. He wanted to live with her, here.

A flight of pigeons passed over the disk of the sun.

Tears streamed down Felion's face, and dried. He had never before, not once, known such joy.

And then Smara came walking toward him, out of a brick wall just down the street, which was not the street outside the artist's house. She looked about shyly, but when she saw him, her face lit with more than the glory of the sun.

He took her hand again, and not speaking they stood together on the height, and watched day move down below the curve of the earth.

Every architecture rose black against its shining. And then the disk was drawn away, and a wonderful softness closed the air, and a magical nocturne of dark, and stars burned up as if nowhere, not in a thousand worlds, had there ever been stars before, or eyes to see them.

"Smara—where did you go?"

"A garden. Not here."

"And I came out miles from that house. Who cares? What does she matter, our mad uncle's artist?"

Hand in hand, they walked the streets as the night filled them. Lamps lit on poles. A breeze blew, sweet with the smell of blossoms from a spring that maybe had not yet begun.

Higher up, they reached the cathedral. The great door was carved with saints and devils, and stood open. An owl flew over their heads.

They entered, and the church was like the stomach of a cliff, it went up for miles. Some service (they had heard or read of such things) must have taken place, for hundreds of candles had been left alight. In the aisle, paper flowers had been scattered.

Felion and Smara separated and went about the body of the cathedral, where no one else was.

Above the altar, a book lay spread on a stand, but when she approached it, Smara could not read the prayer.

Felion, however, found another book in an alcove over a granite tomb. And somehow he read this: "*And the names of the three, who are jointly this demon, are OBLATIC, SAMOHT, and TOLEHCIM.*" Which for some reason made him laugh. And after that the words blurred over and became nonsense, he could not make any phrases out of them.

He and she kneeled under the altar.

"What shall we pray for?" he whispered.

"What is 'pray'?"

He could not answer. He said, "I love you. I always have. If we stay here, we can be lovers."

She turned to him with a look of wonder and happiness. "Could we? Oh Felion, how I'd like that."

They got to their feet and left the cathedral.

Outside, the night was as black as ink now, and the stars had paled before the street lamps, but the big white moon was up, horned, asking only a sky to find its way.

"Where shall we go?" she asked.

"We can go where we like," he said.

So they walked the City.

Paradis has been many things, but seldom heaven on earth. No, Paradys is a venue of shadows, its own books tell us so. But not now, not for these hours. That is the madness of Paradys. It can be also holy, benign, bountiful, and tender.

Outside a café lit by lanterns, Felion and Smara are randomly but charmingly summoned to join in a bridal feast. Delicious food and drink are given them, gratis, food without stones in it or serpents—and wine, not hemlock.

Later they stray up into a park, and here there is a masquerade. Beings with the heads of beasts and birds, deities, and imps. Smara is given a mask of black feathers tipped with nacre, and Felion a sun mask ruffed with gold. They discover that though they cannot read as yet the writing of Paradis, they know its dances, as if taught in childhood.

All night they drink and dance, and later, under a panther black cedar tree, they kiss like the lovers they wish to become, timidly, sensually, carelessly, caressing each others hearts in surprise.

"We can stay here now," he says.

But Smara is abruptly startled. Perhaps the nightingale singing in the tree has interrupted her thoughts.

"But—not yet."

"Why not? What do we leave behind?"

"We must go back, one last time."

"Why?" he says. "Why?"

"I don't know. But don't you feel we must?"

"Yes. I feel it."

"How can we live there?" she says.

"This City takes care of us."

"Tonight it has," she says. "But will it, afterwards?"

They stare across the park, from whose grassy floor one or two absorbing graves rear up their slabs. (Those of whom Paradis has not taken care?)

"Our uncle," Felion says, "trusted himself to this City. I think, in more than one time. He gave himself to it. Let it be cruel, and kind to him. As it wanted."

Smara sat up. She shivered. "I want to go back."

"To what?"

"We were born there."

"All right. Yes. We must."

They left their masks lying, the bird and the sun. There on the grass among the graves.

It was cold before the dawn, the stars were going out.

"Look," he said, "down there, there's the bitch's street after all. Do you see?"

Smara frowned.

They did not, now, touch at all.

On the grass a cloud had formed, showing them, like a temptation, the way back into hell. But they knew hell. They had got used to hell. They went into the cloud.

The labyrinth was freezing and both of them ran through it.

It took a long time, it seemed like hours, to reach the oval heart. And there, panting and dismayed, they halted.

"Has it gone?"

"The ice bird? No, still there."

"I don't mind. It's nothing."

They stood on the glacial floor and he let the guttering torch droop.

"I know how we can be safe in the other City," he said. "We're the heirs of our uncle. And so is she, this artist. We must kill her, Smara. Then we'll have her place."

"Yes," Smara said. It had seemed to her they would never kill again. But she had been in error. "We'll poison her," Smara said, deciding.

Through the labyrinth something roared, and sighed.

They went slowly now, Smara walking just behind Felion. Not careful, not afraid. They were exhausted. The banquet, after starvation, had been too much, for there are those who have died from something like that.

TEN

Paradis

●

What's the use of worrying?
It never was worthwhile,
So, pack up your troubles in your old kit-bag,
And smile, smile, smile.

George Asaf

Brassy chrysanthemums were bursting from the flower bed.
Black ivy had climbed the pedestal of the Medusa, but not
reached, or had avoided, the neck and straining mouth, the
protruding tongue of stone, and the petrified snakes.

Thomas the Warrior was tying up flowers to sticks.

Leocadia stood over him. Suddenly, intrusively, he reminded her of her infantile memory of her Uncle Michelot.

"On your feet," she said briskly. "Soldier."

And Thomas rose, and stood to a stooped, cramped
attention, his chin raised, hands quivering.

"Madame."

"I want a report, Thomas."

"Yes, madame. The chemical attack is over. The losses
were slight. The suits held up."

Leocadia raised her brows. Chemical weapons were ille-
gal. Where had they been used and what was he recalling?
But it was not this past that mattered. Perhaps he was trying
to sidetrack her.

"That's good. Now tell me about the asylum."

Thomas relaxed a little, and looked down at her.

"When I was very young," said Thomas, "a child was
eaten alive in the zoo, by a tiger. No one knew how the tiger
escaped. Its bars, they said, seemed to melt. It was sup-

posedly destroyed, but not in fact. Someone took it away, it lived in a private house. God knows what meat they fed it. Children, perhaps."

"That's marvelous, but not what I asked you, soldier."

"I am," said Thomas, "a voluntary patient. This is my cage, but I don't mind it. I need a cage. I went mad in the service of my country."

(Oh! Uncle!)

"But *are* you mad?"

"Yes. I have a paper to prove it."

"And I'm mad too, am I?"

"Don't you have a paper?" asked Thomas. "You should ask for one. Then you know where you are."

"I know where I am. In the madhouse."

"Not at all. And anyway, that doesn't make you, madame, a correct candidate. Although you may be," Thomas amended, respectfully.

"I believed you thought I was."

"Well, madame, my opinions alter. Part of my condition, of course. Everything does change, here."

"Yes?" Leocadia scented some element of interest, tart as the tang of citrus zest.

"The buildings, for example," said Thomas the Warrior, "move. As the continents do. Slowly. But now in one direction, now another. The hothouse, for example. I recall it was farther off." He indicated the elder asylum. "Gradually, it crept this way. Perhaps to evade capture."

"Capture by what?"

"Who knows?" asked Thomas.

She saw suddenly through him, how he had been young once. And had he ever been a tiger of a man?

"Tell me about," said Leocadia, "the gin bottles. The brown glass ones with the penguin on the label."

Thomas smiled. His teeth were good.

"Penguin Gin," said Thomas. "It's an old rhyme. A corruption of the original slogan of advertising."

"And how does it go?"

"Penguin Gin, Penguin Gin, drink it up, it'll do you in."

"Ah," said Leocadia softly. "And did it?"

"I expect so. Poisonous, apparently. Lead and copper in the pipes, if such there are in the making of gin. Modern gin is completely wholesome and without additives."

Leocadia said, at her sweetest, "So it poisoned them."

"Oh, there was a story I read once," said Thomas, untying a flower from a stick. The stick but not the flower fell down. "An actor, quite famous, from the era of the gin. His name—Martin. He visited the asylum and charmed the patients with recitals from the plays of the great. But later his brain was curdled from the experience. He began to drink gin in low dives of the slums over the river. One evening he died, in a shocking way." Thomas did not look shocked. Nor did he elaborate. He retied the flower to another stick, and breaking the stick that had fallen, he tossed it over the lawn. Then checked. "I always forget. My dog grew old. Have you ever kept pets, madame?"

"Animals are too good for me," said Leocadia.

Thomas seemed pleased by her reply.

He said, "Johanos Martin was killed by Penguin Gin."

Leocadia said, "You're a mine of information today, Thomas. Tell me some more."

"Today I am," said Thomas the Warrior. He pointed at the Medusa's head. "That was a statue of Madness, once. It crawled or hopped here from the old asylum. I found it in the flower bed one morning. The dew was on it."

"Oh, the dew," said Leocadia. "I've not seen it often. And the leaves are falling now. Will there be snow?"

Thomas stared at her, and through her, and away to his chemical battleground which ought never to have been.

"I remember black snow," said Thomas. "Go away. Our conversation is over."

Leocadia said, "Just one further thing. What do you know about the doctors? What can you say about them?"

"Enemies," said Thomas, "who are friends."

"Van Orles," said Leocadia, with distaste.

Thomas turned and walked off along the lawn. The spider man was coming from the other direction, and pawed at Thomas, murmuring he had a good color.

She felt a momentary great loss.

Why had she not thought to paint Thomas, or the head of the Medusa which was not. It was too late now.

She returned uneasily to her room, but her paint had not been removed, her brushes lay where she had left them, and the dangerous bottle, now associated properly with death. The wall of nascent images had not been touched either, yet she was dissatisfied with it and might wish to make changes. (Suitable to the changeable asylum?)

Then again, it was a risk to attempt anything, until she had dealt with her enemy-friend, Van Orles.

Leocadia went to the refrigerator and opened it. Cold.

Leocadia used the button to summon the attendant.

The girl—or one of the girls who all looked the same—arrived.

"I said, I must see the doctors."

"They are so *busy*, mademoiselle."

"I must have Van Orles. It's urgent. It must be Van Orles."

The maid considered her, then went out.

Leocadia drank the pure, cold vodka.

Then she took off her clothes and donned the cream silk housedress.

If parts of the old asylum moved, then too the Residence would move, sliding bits of itself surreptitiously in among the ancient buildings. And the old asylum slunk up over the new, covering it like a rampant animal.

Leocadia left the neck of the dress loose. She brushed her hair viciously. But then there was a noise at the door. She laid down the brush. Her face was smooth as an egg.

Van Orles came in, shut the door. He was all alone, as before, pale and puffy and agitated, trying to be bold and lofty. The warning light around him was like a dry white neon.

"Now, now," he greeted her. He sounded more silly than she had ever heard, like a caricature of himself. He did not light his pipe. He glared, and Leocadia laughed. At that, he backed away. "No violence!" he squawked. "I have warned them, you may be out of control. Someone will come with an injection."

"And spoil our fun?" asked Leocadia.

Van Orles' silly face became a pudding of startlement.

"At least," she said, "you came back alone. I expected you days ago. What a man. What a tease."

Van Orles looked uncertain. He blinked.

"You were unhelpful," he said, "contrasuggestive, previously. You misunderstood my intention and became hysterical."

"I understood everything," said Leocadia. "It was you who made the mistake. Letting me chase you off, when all it required was a little strength. A little manly firmness."

"Your meaning?" demanded Van Orles. His voice was indeed stronger. He sat down on the couch, took out the pipe, and began to toy with it.

"Why should I explain? Are you simple?"

"Be more respectful, Leocadia. In my position—"

"Oh, hush. Such nonsense. Your position is, you're a man, and I am a woman. Do you agree?"

Van Orles assented.

"I was—playful," said Leocadia, sadly, "and you took fright and ran away. He will return, I thought, sweeping all before him. What did you do? You stole my canvases."

"I—"

"Naughty man."

Leocadia offered the unsuspecting Van Orles a grin she had seen displayed in the painting of a famous whore of bygone times. To her irritated unsurprise, Van Orles mellowed immediately, and smiled upon her. What a fool, there in his orb of almost blinding, radioactive light, the light that showed her where the danger was, brighter by the second.

I shall try to see him, she thought, *as a pie with legs and a head.* Just so she would have painted him, if she had been forced to paint him.

"I meant to make a miniature of you," she said. "I meant to paint it on my thumbnail."

Van Orles sniggered.

"What a woman you are, Leocadia."

"Instead I have to paint penguins on the walls. Will it be allowed?"

"Whatever you want, dear Leocadia." Van Orles patted the couch. He slipped the pipe lasciviously into his pocket. "Let me take your pulse."

"Once you brought me a clockwork cat," said Leocadia. "And a fruit that bled."

"Did I, dear Leocadia?"

"Then you won't tell me why."

"Oh, Saume," said Van Orles, "his little experiments. But truly. I don't recall a fruit that—bled, you say?"

Leocadia allowed a button of her cream silk bodice to come undone. Van Orles was riveted.

"My pulse as yours," said Leocadia, "keeps temperate time."

Another button.

"My pulse," said Van Orles, grinning now like the whore, "is quite fast, Leocadia."

And another button. Van Orles puffed, without aid from the pipe. His small eyes bulged.

Leocadia let slip the silk, inch by inch, along the contour of her breast. She waited, and Van Orles made a tiny sound. Then the silk slid over and the globe of whiteness appeared entire, round and pointed too, with its tawny nipple like a sweet or nut.

Leocadia cupped her breast in one hand.

"Do you think," she asked, "I'm losing my looks?"

"Oh—Leocadia—"

Van Orles got up like a stuffed chair on two legs and blundered toward her.

She allowed him to catch her, to rub his face into her

naked breast and rub at the other with his hand. In her turn she caught deftly at the fuming doctor. Through the material of his clothes, the familiar bulge amused her experienced fingers.

Van Orles writhed in her grasp. "Ah—no, Leocadia—"

"And here is the other breast, not a stitch on it. And what is here. Look. My legs are long, don't you think? I've been told they are. And white. But all this bad black hair . . ."

"Ah—Leocadia—I can't—"

"I can feel you moving. What a strong man. You can't resist me, can you?"

Van Orles struggled now, but Leocadia held him firmly in her clever hand, caressing, goading. He stared down between them at her loins, screwed up his eyes, and made a spluttering noise.

"Alas," said Leocadia.

In horror now, Van Orles peered down at the wetness spread upon his upholstery.

"Such is your effect—er—this is—I—" Gravely embarrassed, annoyed, cheated, and overheated, he limped toward her bathroom. "Excuse me."

Leocadia wiped her hands with turpentine and did up her dress.

When Van Orles emerged he was in a worse state, the wet patch now a soaking extravagant monument to vast incontinence of apparently every sort.

"Hurry and hide, before anyone sees," said Leocadia. "If you were noted in your present state—"

"But I—"

"I'm afraid," said Leocadia, "you do look such a sight."

Van Orles' face was now florid. He perambulated about the room in total confusion, staring at things wildly as if they might assist him. Reaching the door he flung himself on it and bolted out.

Leocadia glanced at the wall of ice crags, the dark glimmer of the penguin.

Had she shamed Van Orles sufficiently to safeguard her work?

She walked to the wall, and taking up her brush, loaded it with whiteness whiter than a breast. She was exhilarated. She smiled in a painful rictus, and created mountains.

During the night, Leocadia dreamed that Asra, her hair full of bleeding orange paint, stepped out of the refrigerator. Nothing else happened in the dream, but the next morning, a visitor was shown into Leocadia's room. It was Nanice, her ugly cousin, the inheritrix who had ousted her, put her into the madhouse, *cunning* ugly Nanice, who had had Asra murdered.

Nanice was a picture.

Not that she had grown beautiful, but someone had dressed her as though she might be. Her lusterless hair had been permitted to grow and it had been curled. She had put on a long "artistic" frock, patterned stockings, and unusual shoes. From her left ear dangled a second ear, made of silver, from which, in turn, hung a single polished diamond. Nanice spread her hands in a theatrical way. On her fingers were silver rings shaped like fingers wearing rings.

"How are you?" asked Nanice, beaming.

"Not dead yet. My apologies."

"Always so tragic," said Nanice. "I can't stay long. It was my duty to see you. I've tried before, but they said you were violent. But here I am. Though my friend is below. *She* hates to wait."

Leocadia deduced that Nanice was implying her friend was a female of the intimate sort.

"Art," said Nanice, savoring, "is very freeing. I understand you now so much better." And she removed from her bag a flask, and drained it. Nanice hiccuped.

"And what do you want?"

"To show you how well I am," said Nanice promptly, like a precocious child—and with such a true and perfect malice that it was both naïve and blameless.

"Yes, you're well. But who runs the firm of assassins you hired to dispose of Asra?"

164

Nanice blushed. She said, "How can you speak so lightly of that terrible crime?" She added, "Artistic license can only go so far."

"It was clever of you," said Leocadia, "in a filthy, muddled way. And then, did you wait in the street until Pir and Jacqueline and the others had broken down the door? How much were *they* paid?"

Nanice flounced and the silver earring danced. "Your horrible uncouth friends burst in your door for their own edification. Pir was howling that you ruined his dinner, and that woman Jacqueline said you had run out with a knife in your hand and must be stopped. They hated you, and were impossibly drunk—drunk in the wrong way. They're vandals. But yes, we were on the street, Monsieur Saume and I. I told you, you were being watched. I too was afraid for you." For a moment, Nanice looked her old pious self. Then she smiled, kindly.

Leocadia cackled.

Nanice said, with the air of a canny child changing the subject tactfully, "Robert has been sick in your studio. Robert is always sick, isn't he?"

Leocadia felt a dim rush of fury, but she held herself against it and it sank.

"I have an urge," she said, "to pull off your ear."

"Isn't it wonderful? This jewelry is very fashionable." Nanice was not ruffled. She said, determinedly, "It was such a pity Robert was sick in the studio. I've begun to paint there."

Leocadia now felt wooden, almost lifeless. She had never fainted, but perhaps this was what the sufferer experienced in the instants before awareness went out. Hollow, adrift yet fixed, immutable and flowing. She could not explain this. She said, stiffly, "I suppose you paint little images of pretty ladies you think are yourself."

"Oh no. Not at all. I'm painting a woman with the head of an elk, riding on a horse on wheels."

Nanice did not, as she had vowed, stay long. Her visit had been improbable, as if maybe the friend-enemy doctors had requested her to come: one more test. Or—and for a minute or so after the visit, Leocadia seriously considered this—had she hallucinated Nanice? But would a mad woman conjure something so trite?

Yet the creature who was Nanice was no longer precisely trite. Nanice had taken over the role that Leocadia had played so well and so diligently for thirty years, in the City of Paradis: The bad woman, the eccentric, drinking artist.

Leocadia sat on her couch, turning her brushes in her fingers. On the wall the penguin stood amid the snow, large and three-dimensional.

Leocadia thought about Van Orles coming stupidly outside her body, and the warning light, which had faded as he rushed out of the door. She thought of Thomas, who had begun to look so like Michelot, her uncle, who had been kind to her. And of Asra, of course of Asra, whom she had never really liked.

But Nanice had taken Leocadia's life from her, her persona, her obligations of thought and deed. Her memories? And if Nanice had done that, was Leocadia relieved of Leocadia? No more duties to Leocadia. Leocadia, like a bundle of heavy clothes, rolled up and packed away.

Who am I?

She, whoever she was, rose and went to the refrigerator and took out the tall bottle of vodka. Then, with a sigh, she put it back. She did not really want it. She did not have to drink it.

Who *was* she now?

Strange, she must still paint. The painting on the wall drew her like a window full of light and air. Perhaps, then, like Mademoiselle Varc, and Thomas, she was now a conduit for the madhouse. Whoever she was, she smiled at that. And anointed her brush.

ELEVEN

Paradys

■

Penguin Gin, Penguin Gin,
Drink it up, it'll do you in.

Popular corruption of an advertising slogan

At the Cockcrow Inn, the blackish scum of the alleys had risen to the surface. Outside, the hovels of Paradys clung and clustered to the rainy bank, dark mounds with slitted, small, dull eyes. The interior of the tavern was raucously alight with oil lamps and thick with the smoke of pipes and the foulest cigars. When the tall man entered, heads lifted up into the avaricious glow. They knew him, he had come in before, several nights now. They knew him also as a confidence trickster, a deceiver like themselves, but honored in his profession, as they were not. An actor.

He had not spoken to any of them. Those few who had recognized him had informed the rest. This did not make them like him, or his silence.

When the bar girl had initially told him, pertly, there was no brandy, but only the popular drink, raw gin and sugar, he had taken that. He drank a great deal, and when he was drunk, sitting in his corner, he had muttered things from plays.

Citalbo the poet had once drunk at this inn. It was an old inn, and had had other names.

Perhaps Johanos Martin had been curious about the madman who had given line for line to him. Perhaps he had meant to visit the inn only to see if some essence of Citalbo, or of Citalbo's ultimate fate, had lingered there. Or maybe Citalbo had put a spell of magic upon Martin that had driven the actor down into the inn as another might be sent into Tartarus.

On this sixth night of Johanos Martin's appearance, two of the other deceivers got up from their places and went and sat with him.

"You're the great actor, aren't you? Martin, of the Tragedy."

They spoke of it as if it were a sort of jest, something he might laugh at. But Johanos the priest looked down upon them from the high altar of lamplight and gin and said calmly, "I am Martin."

"Well met," said the bigger of the deceivers, a robber who had once slit throats as regularly as two a night. "Allow us to buy you another drink, monsieur."

"Very well," said Martin. "But what do you want?"

"Oh, the pleasure of your company, monsieur, before we go off on our evening's labors." And with a whistle the cutthroat summoned the bar girl, and bought from her a brown bottle with a penguin on its label. "The best drink in Paradys. This will add fire to your turns on the boards."

"He doesn't lack fire," said the other man, who was only a runner for the squadrons of robbers, capable enough with a club, but mostly good at racing the alleys and climbing up to roofs. "No, it'll cool him, this will. Mixed with snow, this beverage is, and hence the label of ice and freeze."

But Martin was not interested in the bottle. Not yet—he would come to be. Now only the contents had his attention.

They saw to the drink for him themselves, and the runner stirred in sugar.

Then all three drank.

The eyes of Johanos Martin were as ever cold and clear and far away, yet he did betray now a slight nervousness. He said, presently, "You gentlemen are generous. But I hope you don't believe you can rob me. I'm not such a fool I brought any valuables into these slums."

"Rob you? Why, monsieur, what do you take us for?"

Martin smiled faintly.

"This inn," added the big man, "is a kind of fellowship. You're safe enough here. Although, I might say, your great-coat would be worth a little trouble to one or two, if they were to catch you before you reached the bridge."

"Are you threatening me?"

"Indeed not, monsieur. In fact, since you're seen drinking with us, I think you can be easy on your way."

"*He* is the important man," said the runner, indicating the cutthroat. "Like yourself, monsieur. A star in the dark."

"Oh, yes," said Martin, so disdainfully his companions laughed.

And then Martin made a slight move, as if to get up, and a third man who had come into the corner from another table slapped him on the shoulder.

"We like you, monsieur," said the cutthroat. "Don't go. Have some more gin, and then do us a recitation from one of your plays."

Johanos Martin had already been fairly drunk when they first approached him. (And afterward it was speculated upon that he might have been insane, that the jaunt to the asylum had sent him so, or why else had he risked his person in this sink?)

Martin said, "If you wish."

And possibly he was willing to perform, unfed, for a table of creatures such as these, where he would not for the supper tables of the upper City.

But it did not come to reciting. For something in the gin thickened Martin's tongue, as his other tipples had not. Thickened his tongue, and paved his brain with luminous crystal thought that told him he was not in jeopardy, just as all men know they can never die.

Near midnight, they led him out, the cutthroat and the runner and the robber, and two or three others, and together they went along the worm trails of the low bank, through places very old, built over again and again, like some terrible painting that could never be finished.

It was winter, and cold. Above, only occasionally hindered by lamps, the stars were pocks of snow in the sky, the footprints of something, going somewhere. But Johanos Martin did not look at these. He was a great actor but he had no true spirit. Besides, he could not, after all the gin, properly see.

They led him into a house above a coil of the river.

It had not been planned, at least, not in their conscious brains. They let him lie down on a bed, and then they ripped off his precious coat, and then they tied him to the iron bed frame.

When they took from him other clothes, they found his body was pale and hard, in better condition than their own, from his exertions on the stage.

Although drunk, he cried out when, one by one, they invaded him.

In prisons, orphanages, aboard ships, in gloomy watches of the soul, they had found out this means of sodomy, which now they brought and worked out upon Johanos Martin. They raped him many times. Without a single kiss.

And finally it was the runner who thrust into Martin's body the empty gin bottle. Who worked with that upon him.

Inside the anus of the helpless man the four-sided glass neck shattered. (Normally, only orgasm would be sufficiently strong to break such glass.)

Much later, after the deceivers had left him, he was found. And thus, later still, five days later, in a paupers' hospital, Johanos Martin died of a bottle of Penguin Gin. The death was disgraceful, and hushed up.

No last words, or quotations, remained, for in a delirium of agony, such things did not arise.

No one mourned him in particular, yet the spectators of the City did so, for he had held many in thrall that he had not met. The love of strangers.

All that escaped was the rumor he had died of drink.

They did not mind that. It was romantic, tragic: usual.

Hilde woke, weeping in the darkness. Hearing her, some of the others began to cry, and the woman who made sounds made them, over and over, like a bell.

Judit came to Hilde across the moonless black.

"You must be brave. One day, we'll be free. We will go to my country. Or into the heaven of snow, Penguinia. For that is the land's name. Yes, I asked Maque. Don't you recall?"

It was winter, and the room was icy. Hearing Judit's voice, the women whispered and were mute.

"Think of the warm snow," said Judit, "warm as feathers. And the sweet wine."

"I'll never see it," said Hilde.

Judit touched her gently, her head, her neck, her shoulders and hands, Hilde's stomach. There, Judit hesitated.

Like all the beings of the madhouse, Hilde was ferociously undernourished, and she had become very thin. Her hair they had let grow, but it was not as strong as it had been, not springing or bright. The woman Moule had said she doubted it would be worth trying to sell Hilde's second crop of hair. Hilde's belly, where Judit's hands had paused, was hard and round, like the gut of a terrible hunger.

The warders had not noticed, for they did not investigate their charges once novelty wore off, and Hilde, so slight, looked only swollen in the way of malnutrition. But to Judit's fingers, the fact of this pathetic taut belly now became apparent.

Judit, who had been a whore, sat back in queenly stillness. Within the black, Judit closed her beautiful eyes.

"We must prepare."

She bowed her head in a gesture of acceptance and mourning.

Hilde said again, "I'll never see the Penguin Land. The Penguinia. Never. It isn't real."

"Yes. And you will see it, child. Before I do. Penguinia is the country of joy that lies behind this place of pain."

Far off, from the men's dormitory, came the lonely hyena calling of despair.

171

It was not true that Maque had named the Penguin Land. Judit had done that. After the day the actors came to look at them, Maque had been punished in various ways, and he had grown silent. He did not climb on top of the hill of furniture, and one morning the warders dismantled it. They threw the old chairs out into a yard of the asylum.

Citalbo had become quiescent too, and no longer wrote his snatches of verse. The noise from the male dormitory reminded Judit of these silences.

While inside Hilde, a bud had formed, even as the hair grew from her shaven skull. After a few weeks, Marie Tante and Bettile had ceased fastening Hilde into the mad-shirt. As well, for otherwise, they might, even they, have seen.

But the child in Hilde's womb was without quickness. Judit had felt such things before, in her previous existence.

So she prepared, not for the arrival of life, but the advent of death.

Hilde Koster, in the madhouse, carried the dead child of dead Johanos Martin for a little more than five months. Any symptoms of her pregnancy she mistook easily for the constant malaise due to ill treatment, and the minor poisonings to which the inmates of hell were subjected, the lack of any care. And Hilde, who had once been "Little Hilde," was ignorant of biological fact.

So she walked about in the straw of the white chambers, and sometimes in the stone court of exercise, and she slept in the room of the moon, stunned by the horrible cold, a dummy of flesh closed tight around this small lump of mortality.

At the beginning of the sixth month, about fifty days after Martin's death in the paupers' hospital, an incredible quiet sank on the asylum.

The warders prowled the rooms, sometimes slashing at the mad people with their sticks.

"What are they up to?"

Even the ones who crawled in circles or beat at flies did so in utter noiselessness.

172

Into the yard had been shunted a few of the men and most of the women, among them Judit and Hilde.

The day was frigid, like gray quartz, and up into it the biscuity walls rose, gray also in the stasis of the light. Hilde's ruined hair was like a beacon, the only brilliant thing visible, a drop of autumn sun, the splash of a summer fruit. But under the trails of this hair Hilde was a white shivering Madonna of death, who suddenly dropped down, her mouth shaping into the grimace of a mask, a shock too vast for sound.

Figures of ice, the other women stood about, a chorus in a play without words, and without motion.

"Damn the pigs, why don't they make a noise?" demanded Bettile. "Go over, Marie, and hit one of the bitches. Pull that fat one's hair."

The air was stony and silence hurt their ears.

Bettile took a step toward the group of women. And at this instant Hilde screamed in agony.

"Ah, there goes one. Again, again, you slut. Let's hear you!" cried Moule.

And as all the women began to shriek, and inside the block the men yowled like dogs, the warders shook themselves and passed back and forth the brown bottle that only a shameful convulsion could shatter.

Like a hedge, the mad women solidified around Hilde on the ground, and unseen, Judit knelt by her.

There was no time for Hilde to question or protest. Death broke from her in a shattering spasm of water, and of blood.

Hilde screamed, and the women, her chorus, screamed.

The wardresses congratulated them. They smote one or two across the legs. These women skipped and grunted, and then resumed their outcry.

"Old Volpe will hear," said Moule, with satisfaction.

They were tickled.

If Volpe heard, up in his apartment on his country estate, he pretended to himself that these were the cries of winter geese blown inland from the river miles away.

Something tiny and dreadful was squeezed from Hilde's broken body, and lay on the stone ground, linked to her by a silvered cord.

It was if her soul had been squashed out in the shape of a monster.

The warders had gone in, it was too cold for them in the yard. The women stared down on the death that had been born of Hilde.

It was a child, a child in parenthesis, not wholly formed. In color—in color it was like the skin of a pumpkin. An orange child, the product of wronged blood or a damaged liver, the product of a flame that had burned out.

Judit took Hilde's hands.

"It's over," said Judit, as in the back streets of her past she had said it to this one or that, silken girls murdered by reproduction, the task devised of a male god, or demon.

Hilde could not speak. Behind her eyes the sea was drawing away. She lay aground upon the beach. Hollow, adrift yet fixed, immutable and flowing.

"Don't be afraid," said Judit. "You ask me where you are going to? Now you'll see Penguinia."

For a second a light lit in the tidal windows of the eyes. Was it so? After this interval of the impossible, the redemption most human things hope for? Then the light flickered and faded. So swiftly, so clumsily and unbelievably, we must leave.

They were all dead now, the father, the mother, and the child of a cursory act one had wrought on the other.

Only the force and sorcery of the appalling event remained, and hovered there like the smolder of the blood, and was breathed in, through lips, through stones.

The women drew away. There was no more they could do. The ghastly orange gnome of the stillborn must be left for the warders to discover and remove, as the corpse of Hilde, the last door of all slammed on her, must be come on and tidied, roughly and with oaths. A piece of earth somewhere on the premises was kept for such debris. Dead lunatics were cast into sacks and so into quicklime, that there should always be space for the next one.

Outside the walls, about one hundred and thirty meters along the road, and among some desolate somber trees, Tiraud and Desel stood in the dusk before dawn.

Tiraud was grumbling that he had hurt his back, lugging "that bitch." Desel was sullen, in the grip of a sort of agoraphobia, that often came on him when he had to go beyond the asylum precincts.

The burial of the dead female lunatic and her stillborn infant had been gone through on the previous evening. Dr. Volpe had not attended, and it was Desel who spoke the prayer over the dead—which consisted of a drunken burp. The warder had botched up some evidence of the correct event, and then laid the two corpses together in a stout sack. It had been more difficult in earlier years, when Volpeh had nerved himself to oversee all obsequies. Frequently then there had been nothing to salvage for the sinister carts that came up the road, with the morning star.

"Here it is now," said Tiraud, as he gave over the gin bottle to Desel, the Penguin of Joy. "Are they going to haggle again? He's lucky to get it. Such a fresh one, and only a girl. And the abortion's grand for study. Some doctor will delight in it."

Such was the security of the house of madness that they had easily been able to carry out the pitiable sack between them. Those that saw knew and approved their errand.

The cart came rolling up the road, a bundle of shadow, the lean horse pulling it, like some medieval image of Death.

But it was a cheery, leering individual who craned down.

"What have you got for me, eh? Something nice?"

"A young girl of fifteen, only a day old. And a premature child of unnatural coloring," said Desel. "Do you want to see?"

"No, I trust you, *gentlemen*. You know there'd be trouble if you lied."

One bag was hoisted up into the cart. Another, lighter, plopped down.

"It's not enough," said Tiraud. "You promised more."

"Ah, but there, you see," said the carter, "you think this is a rare treat for me, this young lady and her calf. But they're harder to dispose of, these oddities. More questions are asked. And some of my clients turn shy. They'll take a strapping great man without a qualm. But a maiden and a monster baby—who can tell? Why, I may have to tip the lot in the river."

"You bloody liar," said Tiraud.

"Don't waste your breath," said Desel. He took the money bag and began to walk up the road toward the loom of the asylum, which, from this juncture, looked like a weird mansion or fortress, probably romantic, in the half-light and mist.

Tiraud made after him, as if afraid to be left alone and standing in the world

The carter eyed their retreat.

"Mad things," he said to his horse. "Madder than their charges."

As he turned the cart, the sack rattled under the cover. It lay amid sacks of potatoes and swart cabbage, and once he would have taken more care to ensure it was jumbled, the unvegetable death, among his other goods. But this did not matter much now, for the way he went by, into Paradys, was watched by those with whom he was on friendly terms.

It was a winter morning, and the dawn star was very radiant, sending fine shadows away from the standing things of the landscape. A bleak scene, the road and the black trees that periodically flanked it. Here and there a shorn field. Presently there would come gaps where the earth swept down, and the City might be glimpsed, curled around its river and smoking as if deadly on fire. The morning fog preempted the sense of smoke. A silence pushed in against the cart.

"Mad people," said the carter of cabbage and death. "The world's mad. Take me. I could be snoring in bed. Take you, horse, letting me fasten you to this cart."

Something moved in the cart's interior. It might be potatoes tumbling through a sack.

176

The carter cocked an ear. He knew the noise of potatoes.

"What's that, eh?" He did not look back. In his particular trade, he had heard the stories, the corpse that sat up, perhaps wearing the face of a loved one. But the carter had no loved ones. "Better keep still," he wheedled. "I'm taking you somewhere lovely. I am. To help in the pursuance of knowledge."

There was a sound now like a knife slitting a sack.

The carter mused.

"Just stay quiet," he said.

Then something rose up in the cart, and dislodged the cover. Because the dawn star was behind it, its shadow fell across the carter and his lean horse.

"Christ, now," said the carter.

He turned slowly, and looked back.

As he did so, a darkness fell through the air, and then a pallor, and something stung his cheek. It was a snowflake. And in the cart, on top of the sacks, was a huge rock of a bird, black-caped like a nun, with a breast of ice, and an amber blaze against the blade of its beak, which resembled—or might have been—obsidian.

The carter did not know what this creature was, although he had seen it represented somewhere.

In the silence it towered over him. A smell came from it, the odor of spirits, killingly sweet.

During those moments, before the carter could in any way respond, the reins jerked in his hands—the horse began to run.

As the carter clung to the reins and shouted, the darkness seemed to swirl about his head, and the only picture that was with him was of that stone beak like a dagger plunged between his shoulders. Yet he had no choice but to strive with the running horse.

Snow dashed in his face like pieces of a broken moon, a moon made of dead white flesh.

The horse grew tired suddenly and stopped still, the cart juddering and slewing to a halt behind it. With a loud cry, the carter turned again then, and saw the fearful bird thing had vanished from the cart. There instead strewn on the sacks, were the corpses of the dead girl and a little swathed thing that might have been anything small and once alive.

"Now," said the carter, "now, now, now."

He glanced over from the cart, through the flurry of the snow, and saw a hollow place into which they had almost fallen; the horse had stopped on the very brink. Below was a black pool not much larger than a well.

Touching the dead did not bother him, but now he would rather have not. Even so, it must be seen to. The money was lost, but he had cheated them anyway.

He hauled the girl and her fruit off the cart and flung them over into the hole of water. They went without a note, the water closed, and they might never have been.

When he was a mile farther off, the snow ceased. He gazed back and saw it falling still among the uplands and the raped fields. The trees had the shapes of birds waiting motionless, but for what?

Marie Tante moved with her lamp along a night corridor. She was searching for Moule, who always had gin upon her person. Sometimes Moule would slouch up to the room beside the chamber of the Waterfall, and sit behind the glass partition. Marie Tante had often come this way to find her. There beside the lever they would stare into the dim inverted bathtub, with its hanging serpent and the horror chair beneath.

At the unlighted corridor's end, Marie Tante found that she had lost her way. She was not where she had believed she would be. For years she had come in this direction and by this route. She checked in surprise. Here she was on the other corridor, which led to the little cells where newcomers were confined. How could this have happened?

Marie Tante had no imagination. Cruel things stirred her obscurely, but most of the nooks of her brain were closed up, or vacant. It might have been said she was a being who should never have been allowed to live but rather sent back at once to be refashioned, for her life had never gained anything for her, and to others, often, it had been the cause of atrocious evil, misery, and pain.

Lacking intuition, Marie Tante did not consider that something bizarre had occurred, although she knew she should not be where she was. She did not think anything had misled her, let alone that sections of her plane of existence had *shifted*. No, she merely retraced her steps, and got again onto the path toward the Waterfall.

Then however, as she was turning the corner, her lamp cast up a gigantic shadow on the wall high above her head.

Even Marie Tante was arrested.

She stopped, holding the lamp, and looking.

Then she looked back, over her shoulder.

Far off, at the passage's other end, something moved. How its shadow had come forward, and so through her lamp, was a mystery. No other lights burned in these corridors when they were not in use.

Marie Tante could not be sure what she had seen. She took it for another warder, a tall man, and called. But the shape was gone now and the shadow also.

She went on and opened the door into the room that overlooked the Waterfall.

Something black rose up in a lump from the floor.

Moule balanced in Marie Tante's lamplight, hugging herself, pulling faces. On the ground was a smashed bottle. So much for the gin.

"What's up, you fool?" said Marie Tante.

"Something's out there."

"Yes, old Big Feet wandering about, or that other one, Bettile's fancy."

"Oh yes," said Moule, "oh yes."

"What did you think it was?" demanded Marie Tante, irritated by the lack of drink. She toed the shards. In a pool of liquid, the label floated, sodden.

"Do you remember," said Moule, "when we cut off that girl's hair?"

"What girl?"

"The one who died."

"The ginger slut? What of it? You got your share of the money."

"That baby. It was a strange color. Like her hair, the color."

"Tiraud and Desel will have seen to that."

Moule mumbled. She glanced into the chamber of the Waterfall, and squeaked. "Look, Marie."

Marie Tante looked through the glass, where her lamp vaguely shone, and saw that fluid was running from the hose above the chair.

"You dolt. Why work the lever now?"

"I didn't. See, it's in place."

"Some fault in the apparatus," said Marie Tante. "I'll report it."

The smell of the spilled gin was very intense.

"Let's go away," said Moule, spinning about like an unwieldy top.

She clutched at the lamp, but Marie Tante kept a firm hold on it.

"It's the drink," said Marie Tante, "it's addled you."

"Oh, it could be. Let's go back, where the others are."

"Yes, they may have some gin."

Moule followed Marie Tante closely as a scared child, along the dubious, quiet, and unlit passageways.

Down in the courtyard, they passed a pile of furniture, wrecked chairs and parts of tables. Marie Tante seemed to remember it had been stacked up elsewhere, but she did not dwell on this, for obviously the pile had been moved.

The night was bitter cold.

"It'll snow," said Moule, staring up at the bright black hardness of the sky.

"So what? We'll keep warm."

The lunatics had been propelled, for the period of the dark, to their segregated dormitories. In one of the annexes off the vacated rooms of straw, the warders had a fire going. Into this area Moule darted and went shivering up to the hearth.

Desel and Tiraud sat among the men, smoking their pipes and gambling with the cards. Some of the wardresses too had a game, but Bettile was making a shawl, working the smoky wool cleverly, with harsh sharp twists. The hands of Bettile, which had inflicted so many blows, so much hurt, which had struck down Hilde when she would not parade before the actors, and later held her while another shaved the girl's scalp, now forced into the shawl some awful psychometry. Only she, on a holiday, could have borne to wear it.

Tiraud got up abruptly. He had been uneasy since this morning's transaction over the sack.

"Ah, he's off to his harlot," said one of the men. "Give Judit my kiss. Tell her I'll be by."

Tiraud spat. "Judit? That vermin. I'm only going to stretch my limbs."

"Don't take cold. The women's pen has ice hung from the windows."

Tiraud was away, removing in turn the lamp Marie Tante had brought in with her.

The room was sunny with firelight, a merry picture, dear friends gathered at a hearth.

There was the drink also. They portioned it out, starving predators with a kill, who must protect each other for the strength of the pack.

The fire described them, their faces and their hands, the angles of their bodies.

And one by one, it described how they flinched and touched at their cheeks or necks, and then gazed up.

A faint whiteness . . . fell softly through the room.

"Snow," said Bettile, shaking it from her shawl. "The roof's leaking. A fine thing."

"How can it leak? There are the rooms above."

The snow fell. It fell thickly now and swiftly. They got up. It sizzled in their fire and in the lamps, which flickered.

Then the snow stopped, and only the wet spots were on them, like the marks of God.

"Volpe must be told. Some crack in the wall—"

Marie Tante took a swig from her mug. The gin was hot and laced with sugar from the can on the table.

Moule crouched over the fire. She was thinking of a sister she hated, who lived north of the City, and how she might go calling on her very soon.

"Judit, you filthy cow. Open your legs."

The queen of lands beyond Sheba and Babylon lay under Tiraud. Her face of a damask sphinx was exposed to the ceiling of the women's dormitory, and so she saw the snow begin to fall at once. Judit smiled.

"Like it, do you?" said Tiraud. "Dirty whore."

Judit raised her slim hands into the snow, and Tiraud finished in her with a series of unmusical grunts. As he left her, he stood up into the snowstorm.

On all sides the women were sitting up or getting on their feet. They made little noises like birds greeting the morning sun.

"What is it?" said Tiraud. His eyes were wide. He knew perfectly that the snow was falling in the room, out of the ceiling itself.

"Penguinia," said Judit calmly, also getting up, her unclean skirt dropping to hide the vulnerable wound of her body. "The country of ice is coming."

The women were romping now, in the snow, holding out their hands to catch it, rubbing it on their cheeks and eyes. The snow gleamed with its own light, defining the room with a beautiful silver deception, so that the meanness and foulness disappeared, the perspective of pallets and buckets and walls went on forever, becoming hills and distant tumuli. And the women looked young and fresh, lovely, tender.

Tiraud tried to flail the snow away from him like a swarm of wasps. He heard Judit say, "It's warm as roses." He rushed toward the door, grabbing up the lamp, flinging himself outside.

"What is it? It's some trick. Some insane trick of theirs—"

And he heard, from the men's dormitory, a sudden ululation, not the howls of distress or terror that generally went up there, but a full-throated, gladsome baying.

"Desel—" said Tiraud. He ran down the building, down a flight of stairs. A few lamps burned below, and he raced toward the light, for the darkness was not safe.

The snow had not been warm, not to him. He shuddered and sucked his frozen fingers as he ran. Of course, it had only blown in through the broken windows. What was the matter with him? Crazy as the stinking mad people.

He stopped at the bottom of the stairway, amazed at himself. And from the shadow just beyond the lamps, came a statue, walking.

Tiraud identified the creature at once. Laughable and absurd. And yet. It carried with it the soul of the darkness, and all the fearful majesty of some god of the Egyptian underworld. It was the spirit of the gin bottle, and only through that could Tiraud, ignorant of all things but self, have identified it: The Penguin.

It moved as a penguin moves, in a lurching waddle, but very slowly, ponderously, like a juggernaut of the East, a mechanism that had the power of ambulation. It was seven feet in height, perhaps taller. On its white breast the smudge of foxy color. Its head black as stone, black-eyed, and its beak was made to be a weapon of death.

From the dark it came, bringing the dark with it, and went across the space, not heeding the man who watched it, paralyzed, and away again into shadow.

Tiraud's legs gave way and deposited him on the lowest step. Here he flopped, not able for some while to recollect motion.

Then at last he rose, cuddling the stair rail, and next shot himself staggeringly off into the passage *It* had left alone.

And as he wove and sped, Tiraud screamed. The scream burst from him uncontrollably, like steam from a kettle.

He reached the dayrooms of Madness, screaming like this, and screaming he thrust back among his brothers and sisters, the warders. So, being used to it, and to a particular reply, they took him, beat him, knocked him to the earth.

"What now? Are you cracked like the rubbish upstairs?"

"I saw—" said Tiraud, lying at their feet.

"Saw what?"

They did not seem skeptical, but as if they had anticipated this messenger out of the web of the building.

Yet even now he did not dare to tell the truth. He sat and nursed his knees. "Give me a bloody drink." And then he thought of the image on the bottle and pushed the liquor aside. "Someone's out," said Tiraud. "One of them's escaped. Wandering in the corridors." That was all he could say, to them, and to himself, to justify what he had seen. For what he had seen was not real. Then for a moment, he thought of the dead body in the sack. So he reached for the drink after all.

The warders became ferocious, accusing one another. How had one of the lunatics evaded the nightly shutting-up? (And Tiraud, drinking, realized he had not relocked the women's dormitory. He had left them scampering about there and the door had only to be tried—)

And all at once, miles high it seemed, the bacchante cries of women flew through the upper air of the building and unravelled away.

"The beasts are out—all of them," exclaimed Marie Tante, Her eyes lit, and Bettile put down her shawl.

There, in their cave of firelight, they listened. The vision seemed conjured in the room, the mad people in their white rags, flying along the upper corridors, down the steps, across the yards, and up into the other blocks, figures painted by a strange white light, like the moon, with streaming hair and outstretched arms.

Desel strutted forward.

"Idiots! Some of you—you and you, you three there—go to the men's place and see to them. Use your sticks. And you women, you go after those bitches. You'll be sorry, Tiraud, screwing your brains out on that trollop and forgetting the door. I know. Go and alert Volpe now. Why should *he* sleep, the bastard?"

In his downy bed, within his luxurious flat, Dr. Volpe, full of dinner and brandy, was dreaming.

He performed on the piano to a vast audience, up on a great white stage. He felt his genius flood from him.

But it was very cold. His fingers were losing feeling. They stuck to the keys, burning. It came to him, the piano was made of ice, and the stage also was ice. In horror he stared about him, and found he was adrift on the ice floe in the midst of a coal-black sea by night. And from the sky rang hammering blows.

These blows woke him. He lay huddled, the warmth slipping back into his body, gradually understanding that someone smote on the door. His housekeeper had gone to the City on some errand. He would have to attend to the door himself. And what could it mean, this nocturnal racket, but only trouble?

Still shivering, he lit his lamp, and fumbling himself into his dressing gown, he sought the door.

The warder Desel and some other man stood there.

"The lunatics have escaped, doctor, and are running all over the buildings, perhaps the grounds."

"What?" said Dr. Volpe.

Desel repeated his cryptic news. Volpe sensed, correctly, that even in agitation, Desel drew enjoyment from Volpe's fright.

"They must be caught," said Volpe superfluously. "They may damage things—they may harm themselves."

"The others are going about, doctor, trying to capture the wretches. They will, of course, be as gentle as they can, but restraint or blows are probable."

"No, no," feebly said Volpe.

Desel glowered with authority.

"They're violent. Suppose they get out on the road?"

"Ah . . . yes."

Volpe drew back into the room. He strained his ears but heard nothing at all, not the faintest cry.

Desel said, "We'll inform you, doctor, of events."

"Yes," said Volpe. "Good, trustworthy men. I can leave this—in your hands."

When he had shut them out, Volpe bolted and locked the door. He hurried to the window.

Something pallid flitted among the chestnut trees—or did he imagine it? He was sensitive and now his nerves were bad. He could no longer see anything moving there.

A loud crack caused him to jump. He gazed transfixed at the hothouse. Some panes of glass had given way, he could not see them, yet he felt the hiss of coldness coming in upon the winter fruit.

Because he had been woken, the brandy he had drunk was affecting him uncomfortably. His heart beat in a rattling way in the midst of his frame.

There was an impure and acid smell in the room.

Dr. Volpe turned, tracing the smell at once to the ewer of water standing beside his plants. He went to the ewer, sniffed at it. He recoiled. One of those men must have played a joke on him. It was in bad taste, and besides he could not think how it had been done, since neither of them had entered the room. The ewer, however, was full of their disgusting gin.

Volpe wanted to open the window and pour the muck out but was afraid to. Perhaps the mad people were on the roof and might, somehow, reach down—

And perhaps one of the mad people had got into his apartment as he slept, and contaminated the water.

Volpe was immobilized by terror for some minutes.

Finally, trembling, he lit the other lamps in the room, and then in the bedroom, and armed with the poker from the dead fire, he stole around, parting curtains and peeking into closets.

No one was there, and nothing but the ewer had been disturbed.

A dreadful compulsion made him go at last to the ewer, dip in one finger, and lick it. The flavor was like venom; it made him gag, as he had known it would. He raised the jug and bore it into the bath chamber, pouring it away through the drain of the bath. Then he employed the tap, and from its nozzle ran a stream of stuff that stank just like the gin, that surely *was* gin, although how could it be?

Volpe shut off the tap and panted back into his sitting room.

In the lamplight, the birds' eggs and the growing plants glistened oddly, as if they had been coated with moisture or frost. And on their pins the butterflies flamed, and the remains of the butterfly that had crumbled were like metallic dust.

Reaching the male dormitory, the three men found the door was shut and locked. The calling of the women had faded, and they had seen none of them. Marie Tante and her crew would take care of this.

There was no longer any noise, either, from the male dormitory.

Armed with their sticks, and certain other implements, iron hooks, and so on, the warders decided to go in and effect a lesson on the madmen who had howled of their own volition.

The door was undone.

The long room, substantially exactly the same as that which housed the women of the asylum, was undisturbed. But by their pallets the men stood, every one of them, voiceless and intent, as if ready. Even the worst cases, who seldom kept still even asleep, were poised and altered. The man worried by insects did not hit out at them, the swaying man scarcely moved. On the grinning face of the man who grinned, the pain had been mitigated by a curious attention.

"What's this row, then?" asked one of the warders, irrationally, of the silence, and a couple of others hefted their sticks and hooks.

Thin as the thinnest rope, the mad sailor, Maque, walked forward from his bed place.

"I've sailed the seas," said Maque, "but I never saw the cold country of the snow."

"Shut up, you," said the foremost warder. "Or do you want a bit of this?"

Maque leapt up in the air, straight at the warder. Maque's bony hands and nails like claws tore furrows in the flesh of throat and face. And as the warder raised his stick, shrieking, his fellows roiled forward. But in that moment a colossal sound passed through the building, through atmosphere, through stone, and through every atom in between. It was the resonance of an enormous organ, or perhaps the music of the arctic wind that threaded some hollow pipe of ice floating in eternity.

After the sound, the wind itself rushed across the room. It blasted against the warders and threw them back, and they careered about with their eyes starting, yelling at the cold savagery of it, the sticks and iron ripped from their frozen hands.

Where they fell, the lunatics sprinted by and over them. As if at this signal, the prisoners darted out to freedom.

Of the felled warders, the two that could got up and pursued the madmen, shouting and cursing. One man, whose leg had been snapped, pulled himself along the corridor, begging his comrades not to leave him, but when he reached the turn of the passage a huge shadow went by and the warder buried his head in his arms, gibbering.

Marie Tante, Bettile, and their sisters could not find the madwomen. In small groups, they spread out through the buildings, searching. They too carried lamps and sticks, and a few had brought mad-shirts, in preparation.

From outside the blocks of the asylum, it was possible to see these lamplights passing up and down the windows of the buildings, and now and then over the yards, which gave the bizarre impression that parts of the masonry were shifting about, going from spot to spot, crossing over one another.

Sometimes a shout would echo down the night, but it carried no meaning except alarm or rage.

No snow had fallen on the outer ground, or if it had, it was invisible. Only the great cold was there, and the moonless shine of stars.

In the last block, Dr. Volpe's apartment burned with frantic light. Once or twice he appeared at the window. He had heard a peculiar sound but now believed it was only his overwrought nerves that had caused it, inside his own head.

Small pieces of glass from the hothouse lay on the grass like fragments shed from the duller stars.

The captives of the asylum strayed down, maybe from force of habit, to the rooms of straw to which they were herded by day. They had never been there in the dark.

Citalbo met Judit, and Maque appeared with blood under his nails. The rest followed them.

Uncoerced, they went into the annex where the warders had been sitting at their fire. This room was warm and magical, and the people called lunatic wandered about in it, examining the things their jailors had left lying, the cards and pipes, and the hideous shawl, which Judit cast suddenly into the flames of the hearth.

They sipped, too, at the abandoned mugs of gin. But their systems had been denied alcohol so long they did not like it, indeed some wept and spat the gin onto the floor.

All about them, the madhouse was rife with searchers and destroyers, but here in this firelit heart they were in sanctuary. Had their warders returned here, they would have found these freed slaves easily. But they did not return. Only darkness and whiteness, with a flash of amber, came and filled the entry.

Then the people were afraid.

But Citalbo said, "No. This is the hour."

And Maque said, "They're mild birds. They don't do harm."

And Judit said, "He's like a king, a great monarch. We must go with him."

And so, as the Penguin moved from the entrance way, they went out, all of them. And in their path, right across the rooms of straw, there was a wall. And on the wall was a painting. It was of ice floes and sheets of ice, and beyond the ice were mountains. A marigold glow hung over it, and there before its face the Penguin was, as if it had been painted too, onto the wall.

189

"Penguinia," said Judit. "I'll give up my land, to be there."

There are instants of immeasurable beauty. They evolve and are and cannot be argued with.

Out of Penguinia came the organ note that shook the asylum to its roots, and next came the wind of the snow. But it was not cold. It was warm as the fire on the hearth and much, much sweeter. And as this happened, as Penguinia breathed upon them, the wall of the painting opened, and became actual, like the gateway into a garden.

So they saw the soft, warm snows, and the trees blooming up from them with their apricot and orange fruit, and the sun purred on the ice, and a stream bubbled like champagne. Flowers grew in Penguinia, and beyond the slopes of white, a golden sea sparkled.

Some broke away at once and ran and ran through and ran out into the landscape of this country of heaven.

"I dare," said Citalbo. "Let's go there."

And Maque and Judit and Citalbo walked up to the edge of the snow and stepped over among the flowers.

Then the others came after, all of them, the ones who slouched like sad apes, and the ones who shook and the ones who had cried alone in the night for years. And as the soft ground of Penguinia received them, they looked up in wonderment.

Judit bowed to the spirit, the great Penguin, and then alone hastened over the snow toward the sunlit sea, where the seals were diving and descending like mink ribbons.

"Worlds set like suns," Citalbo said, "and rise like suns. That's mathematics."

"There'll be huge white bears," Maque said, "and little white foxes."

"But kind," Citalbo said, "here."

Behind them the rooms of straw had become only a hole of darkness, which was dissolving.

Maque looked back.

Through the aperture, some of the warders appeared. They had blundered into the lower building from the yard. Marie Tante was there, and Tiraud. They gaped at Penguinia.

"Close the gate, quick," said Maque.

On the platelike faces of the warders was a look that had nothing to do with reason or duty. It was a gaze of fury and jealousy, of wicked, blind human bestiality, which had been cheated.

But then the hole back into hell went out, like a momentary flaw in sight. It was gone, and the world was gone, and there was simply *here*, which would be kind.

Only Tiraud ran at the empty space and smashed at it with his stick. Only Tiraud roared.

Marie Tante had already dismissed the mirage. As what? She did not have the wit to specify.

Moule sniveled, thinking she had gone mad.

While all across the buildings of hell, the others bounded up and down, with their lights and instruments of hurt, seeking, stumbling, and in his flat, the collector of murdered birds and butterflies, Dr. Volpe, tapped at his piano in objectless fear. And the walls and planes, the walks and yards and lawns, slid and shifted this way, that way, and abruptly froze to stillness.

"What's that noise?" said Desel, pausing on a stair.

"I smell gin," said Bettile suspiciously.

Dr. Volpe stared inside the piano lid.

There was a trickling, and then a flow, like a thousand taps. That was all. And then there gushed from every pipe and drain, from every cup and bottle, out of every crevice and pore and tiniest crack, the Wave.

It reeked. It reeked of gin. It was gin.

Iridescent and limitless, it crashed through all the lower chambers, and up all the stairs. It plowed across the rooms like a liquid wind of steel. The lamps sizzled out.

They heard and saw it come, and *smelled* it come. This climax of poisonous despoilment.

There was a handful of seconds, during which not one moved, but everything in them lunged and boiled in an

191

attempt to keep its life. But the very smell of the jolly fluid, on which they had sustained themselves, was vilely overpowering. Tears ruptured from their eyes and nostrils and dribbled, salivating helplessly at the onset of death. For death came, it swept in on them like the tsunami, the tidal breaker of an ocean. The putter-out of light.

Then they screeched. Each and all of them. They had been made one.

Drooling and retching, tears and snot running down their faces, they tried to get away before it, but the Wave caught them, effortless, and swallowed them. They were lifted off their feet, turned over, bobbed up to the very ceilings and peaks and slammed there.

Full. They were filled. Bellies, sinuses, lungs, arteries, blood. Brains. Spasms uncontrollable and useless convulsed bodies, drowning in liquid fires, everyone trying to heave inside out and so expel the invasion. Mindless, soundless sneezing, spewing, acrobatic in the wet globe of rushing spirit. *Drowning*. Gin skins.

They gave up their ghosts through their mouths, and there came then the last squeezed fistful of seconds, during which hallucinations settled on them, devils and nightmares, the beasts of the labyrinth of an alcohol-drenched mind, the children of the Minotaur.

And so Marie Tante was skinned in slices by bald, taloned things, and Moule was choked with skeins of hair, and Bettile beheld swimming toward her the net of her shawl, which tore off her breasts and reached in for her heart, and Tiraud lay on a dissecting table, conscious, while his organs were prized out of him, and Desel was stretched on a rack until he broke.... And in his apartment, Dr. Volpe was trying now to burst open his window, and it bit at his hands, and so he witnessed his plants had hold of him like things of the sea, and as they held him the eggs hatched, and out erupted prehistoric birds to peck his eyes and liver, while the butterflies flew in the flood of gin and scratched him with their pins.

When the twenty-one overseers of hell were dead, the Wave sank swiftly down, leaving only its tidemarks on the walls, and here and there a body, stuck against the plaster, or on the stairs, or the floor.

The Wave melted and only the night replaced the Wave. And presently the moon rose over the pristine buildings, and the lawns and the hothouse, which had grown cold. The moon was round, and white as snow.

The penguins waddled and preened on the flowery ice. The people played.

The man who was tormented by insects held out his hands, and the butterflies that now flighted around him sat like fiery papers on his fingers. The man who swayed was dancing. The woman who mourned, sang. The man who grinned was solemn, not a trace of a smile, as he paced beside a small pale fox. Citalbo walked with bears. Maque sailed the golden sea.

On Judit's head was a starry crown.

It was dawn forever. And a day.

TWELVE

Paradise

▲

See, the Minotaur has two daughters; call them
"Left" and "Right." Sometimes.

John Kaiine

"Do you remember our uncle's dog?" Felion asked Smara.

"No," she said. "He can't have had a dog."

"Yes, a feral dog from Clock Tower Hill. It lived with him to a very old age and died in its sleep."

Smara laughed. "I do remember now. He said it could purr."

They sat facing each other, over the woven carpet they had brought to sit on. They were at the heart of the ice labyrinth, had been there most of a day, picnicking on bottles of river water, fried lentils, and dry bread soaked in wine.

Above, the shadow of the ice bird hung as if against a starry night. Both of them had noted this. The torch burned steadily. It did not seem the ice had melted at all.

"When we were born," said Smara, "we were energy. But it became flesh. It became *us*. If we'd died at birth, where would it have gone?"

"Back into our mother."

"But she might have died too."

"Why do you ask?" he said. "We didn't die."

"I dreamed someone dropped our mother into a well," said Smara softly.

"She threw herself off a tower."

195

They drank the water of Lethe, and stared at the patterns in the carpet.

Each of them recalled the hours in the other City, the amber light, the sun and moon and stars. But all this seemed far off. And what they had to do—that was farther still, perhaps unreachable. Both had killed so often, it was nearly a commonplace, a piece of work that required cleverness, quickness, application, and toil. But simple. Now, eventually, they had arrived at a killing that would be momentous: the murder of their uncle's heir, which would cement their chance in the world beyond the maze.

Sometimes Felion, or Smara, would have got up, but some laxness or nervous gesture of the other's put them back again.

At last he said, "Shall we do it now?" Smara said, "Suppose she isn't there?"

"We must want her to be there. We must want to meet with her. And if she isn't, we must wait in the house, for however long it takes her to come back."

They rose.

Smara wore the earrings Felion had recently brought her, and he the ring she had awarded him.

They had agreed. They would use, since it was the term of poison, the means they found to hand in the artist's studio, for these would surely be unique, unlike anything they had employed ever before.

They left their carpet and their picnic lying, and walked out along the left-hand way, into the labyrinth.

"If we're separated," he said, "we must each try to find the other. By thinking of the other. That seems to be the way. We always do find each other again."

"And we're always parted."

They did not touch, they did not hold hands. They carried nothing with them save the torch.

The labyrinth seemed, now, very silent. No visions had assaulted them when they first came in, and none flowered out on them now. They might have been in an ordinary cold, weird corridor, some vein of their uncle's house, going nowhere very special.

And then they turned a turn and found the exit point before them.

"Can you see anything out there?" Felion asked Smara.

"No," she said, "just darkness."

"Yes, only darkness. No moon. No stars. We'll have to trust it. It seems to demand that. Don't be afraid."

"I'm not," she said. "Only cold."

He put down the torch. They went forward, without faltering, side by side. And side by side they passed through the exit of the labyrinth. And were parted from each other as day from night.

The woman was there. Before him. In the studio. She had her back to him, and she was naked.

Felion kept entirely still.

Overhead was the skylight. Black, moonless. And the lights in the studio were so bright he could not see the stars.

But the woman was clear. Her white body and long fleecy hair.

And as he watched she turned about. She saw him at once, but in a misty way, amused rather than amazed. She was drunk or drugged. In her hand was a tube of orange paint, with which she had been daubing her slim, smooth body, shapes like islands.

"Well, hallo, hallo," she said to Felion. "Have you been hiding here long? Have you enjoyed the show? My, I thought the door was only set to recognize *me*. And all the while she's had another secret lover." The girl paused. "I'm glad I told them all those lies now, about her. About her violence. What a cat. She deserves it." She shook her hair. "But you're a real beauty. Oh, yes. Who are you?"

"Felion," he said.

"Felion. What a pretty sound. And I'm Asra."

"So that's your name," he said.

She wiggled the tube of paint down her skin, leaving a glowing trail like a snake of alien blood.

"Do you like my canvas? It's a new gimmick, edible paint. It tastes of *oranges*—yum. I thought she might like to lick it off. But now that I've seen you, perhaps you'd like to? Just think, if she comes back and finds us together. You know what a beast Leocadia can be." Asra, Felion's uncle's heir, the artist in her studio, dipped the edible paint against, between, her loins, and squeezed. "Won't you try a little?"

Felion moved toward her, and reached on the way the table with its paraphernalia of materials.

Another tube of the orange paint was there.

"And is this edible," he asked, "or toxic?"

"Oh that's the real stuff. No, leave that alone. Look, there's plenty here. Why don't you let me put a little on you?"

Felion left the table, the other tube of toxic paint in his hand. He came up against Asra, against her satin body, smearing it slightly, and then stepped around her, behind her. He slid his left hand about her silky throat and up over her lower face. In a second he had blocked off all her air, and she was kicking and writhing, her feet off the floor. He let her drunkenly struggle for half a minute, not exerting enough force to choke but only enough to stifle.

Then he slapped away his hand from her and pushed instead the opened tube of toxic paint between her lips. As her mouth gaped wide to gasp the air, he compressed the tube strongly.

The finesse of many murders had made him more than competent.

He held her as she convulsed, as he had never held a woman in the death throes of love.

When Asra, his uncle's heir, was dead, he raised her and hung her over the easel in the middle of the room.

He stood a moment, taking in the picture that she made.

Then he walked over against the wall.

"Smara!" he called.

The wall opened, and there, simplistically, was the way back into the ice. Smara must be there. Or she would meet him there, as before.

He glanced behind him, but the studio was already reeling away, swaying and bucking, on a chain of light. He seemed to have lost hold of it, all connection to it. He had a sense of panic—but then he only stepped over into the labyrinth; he had done what he came for. He must find Smara. Then they must return at once, outside the house. They must go back to this City for good, the City of the sun and moon, and nothing would stop it. They could never be separated again.

Even as he emerged into the heart of the ice (so quickly he got to it), Smara ran into the space after him, as if she had only been concealed somewhere in the wall, and it was a game. She was giggling.

"I did it!" she cried. "Without you."

"What did you do?"

"I killed her," said Smara, happily. "And then I came here, to look for you."

Felion said, "Wait. You killed her?"

"I went straight into the studio. The room you described, with the skylight. I think it was afternoon. She was blind drunk, going about in front of a canvas smothered in daubs of paint. There was a bottle of white spirit I knew was poison. I ran at her and tipped half of it down her throat before she realized what was happening."

"But Smara," he said, "*I* killed her."

"You?"

They stood as if frozen in the heart of ice, in the silence, and in the shadow, for neither he nor anything had bothered with the torch, which had gone out. They stood and stared at each other.

"If we both," he said, "killed a woman in that room, which of us killed *her*?"

Smara said quietly, "Or did neither of us kill her?"

"We must go back," her said. But they started together as if magnetized.

And from above came a huge crack of noise, like the thawing of a frozen sky. Stars rained over them, but they were stars of ice.

Felion and Smara looked upward, and framed by a smothered darkness, like Paradise, they saw the bird of ice, a column with a great beaked head, leaning over on them as if it meant to speak. Neither of them uttered a sound. They flung their arms about each other, and through their skulls swirled the images of their lives, bright as sparks, and over these a closing curtain thundered like a wave.

The ice statue crashed directly onto them, crushing their bodies together, so that the bones of each broke through the other's skin and mingled, and next mashing them down deep into the ground surface of muddy glass, from which their picnic had vanished. The bird beak of white obsidian went through their hearts, and pinned them one to the other, and pinned them to the earth. The bulk of the bird thing cracked on them like a boulder, covering them, stoppering them beneath into the floor of the labyrinth.

When the silence came again, it was imperfectly. For it was full of a faint tiny sound, like dripping water. The shadow and the cold wavered and dulled, and a sort of rain began to fall, but there was no one to see or hear it. No one to wonder what it might be. If it was anything at all.

EPILOGUE

Paradis

Boys and girls come out to play,
The moon doth shine as bright as day.

Nursery Rhyme

Between waking and sleeping, twilight illusions would come to her, not really dreams. As she grew older, she liked these times, and sought them out. From them she had garnered much of the material that now she painted, but always the backdrop of these pictures was the same. She had come to love and want to paint the same vision, over and over, only subtly altering it here and there, adding, as years passed, the diamonté trees and glimmering fruit and bonbons, the animals, the ship on the sea, and the dancers on the shore.

There had not been an exhibition of her work for two decades, and *then* they had said, "Leocadia's senile. Does that still happen? Look, how repetitious and trifling."

Nanice's one great masterpiece was still at the academy near the Observatory, the modern building with the dragon of bronze on its roof, and antique graves paving the garden at its foot.

Leocadia would cackle when she though of Nanice. After all, Leocadia was now ninety years of age, and to cackle, finally, was quite becoming. Her gray hair was still thick, and still kept its obstreperous curl. She wore it loose to her waist. The rest had gone the way of all flesh, shrunken and fallen. And yet a young photographer who had come to visit in the autumn had obviously found her beautiful, not sexu-ally, but spiritually, in her second youth before the coming of age of death.

Leocadia did not miss sex, she had had so much of it—precisely enough, in fact—in her earlier years. Only during her sojourn at the Residence had she been celibate, and that omission had only lasted nine months, the length of a pregnancy.

The scales had dropped from her eyes. And what scales! After she had painted the penguin and the ice floes on the wall. A day, two days, ten, went by, and gradually, softly, it came to her that everything had been a delusion. She discov-ered her canvases then, stacked up among the books in the alcove library, where she must have placed them, hidden them from herself, pretending that Van Orles had done it as a punishment. Indeed, it was Van Orles who congratulated her on the wall painting. He had followed her work for years, and this, he said, was an honor for them, and a great pleasure, to have an original landscape by Leocadia le Vey to enhance the room. It would be therapeutic for whoever was lucky enough to be put in here.

Van Orles was not ugly. Nor were any of the other doctors. Saume's teeth were even and white, Leibiche did not have pimples, only one coy beauty spot beside his mouth. Duval was extremely, nearly stupidly handsome. What had she been seeing? She asked them.

"Ah, we were your enemies, posing as friends. Beware of Greeks bearing gifts. Your line of defense, mademoiselle, was to remake us as monsters."

When she told Duval she had found him ugly (which she could not resist doing), he blushed, like a plain woman complimented on loveliness. Obviously, no one could ever have said this to him before.

When Leocadia had not drunk anything alcoholic for seventeen days, they urged her to take a little wine. Her system was not ready for such drastic deprivation after the influx that had gone before. So then she had a glass of wine with her dinner, and a little gin in the afternoon. She fancied gin. It was totally pure, colorless, not like the liquid that had been in the mysterious brown bottle.

They were intrigued by the bottle. Sometimes, they said, the Residence guests did find things of historic interest. Did she wish to keep the bottle? Leocadia kept it.

They began to let her go for walks in the countryside, and presently to journey by car to the City. A doctor always went with her. When she could, she chose Van Orles. She had begun to find him very attractive, better than Duval, who was like a classical god, a sweet too pretty to eat. Van Orles was muscular and brawny, with thick dark hair. He did not speak in the peculiar threatening way she had believed, and when they talked, answered her freely, offering his past among a family of cooks, and how he had made his way with difficulty into his profession. No white neon, like a rampant moon, shone around him now, nor did it with the others. She did not know what the light had been, save it was a warning—of her own misjudgment, presumably. She could not be sure how much she had only imagined, although evidently many scenes had not occurred at all. She thought this entertaining rather than unnerving. Perhaps things had taken place on some other plane, in some parallel world. There Van Orles had harassed her, and there she had made a fool of him. But not, certainly, here. Now Leocadia did try to seduce Van Orles. And she began by telling him of the delusion, what she thought she had done, baring her breast and forcing him into a premature ejaculation that had spoilt his trousers. Van Orles lowered his eyes. "Naughty Leocadia," he said. And then, when she kissed him, gently, "You're a wonderful woman, and I'll admit I've had a crush on you for years, before even we met. But how can I now? You've been, and still are, my patient. I'm selfish. I'd lose everything. And you'd only laugh." He did kiss her back. She never forgot his kiss. It was strong, courteous, amorous, frightened. "Of course I'm afraid," he said, "Look what could happen, out in this field." For she had made the car stop on the way to Paradis. She did not do so again.

She briefly hated the City. It looked unfamiliar, as if it had been up to something while she was away.

"For a long while," he said, "you've been out of touch with yourself, and everything."

She insisted she had not killed Asra. But recalling the episodes of accusation swathed in light, she did not think he would say that she had. And he said, "No. Unfortunately the murderer has never been found. But it wasn't ever thought to be you. You seemed to think so, from time to time. But even your cousin, Nanice le Vey, was quite belligerent on the matter of your innocence."

The pastel cravats suited him, mild on his tanned, bold shyness.

She had misinterpreted everything, but something in the painting of the penguin and the snow had released her. Why and how? They spoke to her of projection, of unknown country being the cipher for death and so of rebirth. She knew the moment she had begun to be reborn—or at least the moment of death. Nanice had done that for her, by taking Leocadia's role. They would not admit they had tried to use Nanice as a catalyst, only that she had been an insistent visitor they had at last allowed to call.

Leocadia herself experimented with the others, the bizarre people of the Residence. Mademoiselle Varc had reached the end of her treatment, which she had been receiving for a premature senility. She was now quite sane. Soon she would travel far away. She sat in the summerhouse with the white and cinnamon windows, and held Leocadia's hand. "You were so patient with me. Do you know, I'm a journalist? It's almost a surprise to me, I can tell you. I can't wait to get back, I've missed so much. Thank God, they've made me myself again. And did I call you Lucie? She was a dear child. No, not my friend—my daughter, who died. But yes, there are five others. Each has a different father, and all are fascinating. But there, the proud mother."

Leocadia mentioned the wooden dolls and the amber necklace Mademoiselle Varc had drawn from the rubbish tip in the yards of the old asylum.

"But I believed *you* put them there—for *me!*"

Leocadia said, "Oh. You've found me out."

It was then that truly she began to slot together all the pieces. Having no guide, she did not know for sixty years what they formed.

She only said to Van Orles, then, "The asylum itself is mad."

"What else?" he said.

Thomas the Warrior would no longer speak to her, and perhaps never had. Van Orles explained that Thomas was a war hero from a campaign seldom spoken of, erased from government files. He was almost unreachable, but he feared dogs. He would never reveal why. He also feared high towers, apparently.

The spider man, too, was not as Leocadia had thought him. His odd way of moving was due to a spinal injury that had proved incurable. He was afraid of anyone who walked upright—almost everyone—and Leocadia found that if she sat down immediately he appeared, he would come and talk to her. He was a poet, and the most exquisite phrases poured from his lips. One evening, before the sun had quite gone and they were expected to go back to their rooms, Leocadia lay in his arms under a cedar tree, out of sight of everything but the biscuit blocks of the old madhouse. Nothing happened, but she knew she had made him glad. She knew, greedily, he would put her into a poem.

For by now she was greedy. She ate roast chicken and potatoes with cream, mandarin tarts, orange caviar.

They let her go in the very early spring, before anything but bark was on the trees.

She had by then heard about Nanice.

Leocadia's cousin, who had taken on Leocadia's life, living in Leocadia's house, adorning herself as an artist, painting in the studio, drinking in Leocadia's style. She had been infected, as if the house were full of a plague called Leocadia. Poor Nanice, she had led such an exemplary and careful existence until then, incarcerating Leocadia from moral concern, or was it moral jealousy and wild hunger?

Nanice, in her Leocadia role, was painting in the attic one day, dead drunk. Her works were a disaster, she had no talent, but Nanice had not noticed this. Nor did she notice in her inebriated confusion that the bottle she gripped contained white spirit and not vodka. She had drained it. There was no hint she had intended suicide. Her lover, a young woman of slight mind, had told how Nanice was full of life. By which it was thought she meant full of money.

In the death seizure, however, Nanice fell headlong onto her current canvas, and the resultant chaos, when it was peeled from beneath the corpse, had become a sensation of the City.

It was exhibited at the academy, and popular acclaim kept it there. In its queer and ragged runnels, its smears and gobs of color, Paradis read impassioned and macabre secrets. Dead, Nanice became one of the most famous artists of her era, far eclipsing Leocadia le Vey.

Even so, the house near to the old wall was left vacant, and Leocadia moved back into it, and her inheritance returned to her without hindrance. There had been no plot. Asra's death had driven her out of doors from an already wavering mind. Though why was in some ways a dilemma. Again, sixty years would need to elapse before it would seem that possibly she had had to go mad, had been needed to go mad, in order that she enter the Residence, and there perform the magical spell upon the wall.

Emerging from the asylum was far worse, more uncomfortable than emerging from insanity. Now she must leave her true friends who were not her enemies. She did so. She shut them all out.

She scoured all trace of others from the house. She made it white, with sofas and drapes of snow, carpets of simulated polar bear fur, mirrors like glaciers. Her studio she filled with treated ice sculptures that did not melt, holding ivory daisies, marigolds, lilies, ivy.

It was said in Paradis she was still mad, had got worse.

Although she took lovers and ate dinners and strolled in the City, she closed herself in, every month more and more.

She painted huge canvases of a land of ice, with mountains of ice. And as she picked her way across this snowy id, she reached the sea, and there she painted the meeting of a black-haired queen with a young girl who carried in her arms a child. And Leocadia painted also ships with carrot sails, and seals, and dancers, and butterflies. And still, she did not know why.

The photographer who came to Leocadia in what she supposed must be her old age was in love with her painting (like Van Orles—now, alas, long dead) and with a little novel she had published, about a land she called *Penguin*.

They sat in Leocadia's white salon, drinking orange-flower tea and tiny goblets of crystalline gin.

She showed him the brown bottle with the four-sided throat and the label.

"Is it awfully old?" he asked.

"Older than I am."

"Oh," he said, "but you're young."

"It was the time I went mad," she said. "I found it in the grounds of the lunatic asylum."

He said, "You're one of the truly sane."

She showed him the pictures, all the views of *Penguin*, some with proper penguins stamping humorously about the ice. And sometimes there was a tiger-colored moon, very bright.

"Have you heard about the penguin spirit, Koodjanuk?" he said. "I think you must have. The ice peoples invoke him to heal the sick."

"Yes, I must have," said Leocadia. Something clicked loudly inside her skull. One of her elderly bones shifting, perhaps. "Also a vengeful spirit," she said vaguely.

"Maybe all spirits are, if you go against them." He smiled at the penguins, which were small and playful. "And who is this girl—may I ask?—with ginger hair?"

"I saw her once," said Leocadia firmly. "She must have died, because she was a ghost."

And Leocadia thought, *How wise and elegant I've become, with ninety years*. And again, click.

"But here she is too," said the young photographer, "and here, dancing with a young child—it's charming."

"God knows who she is," said Leocadia. She thought, *But I know her really. She's the young virgin at the Sabbat, before the cocks crow. Through her the power comes, to remake things.*

She thought, *And through me. Something I did. I made a world. I gave it life. And the sun and the moon.*

Leocadia dreamed that one day she would be painting among her solid statues of ice and flowers that did not die, and a touch would come on her shoulder, or something harmless would be thrown at her neck. And she would turn to find the path into *Penguin*, which she had earned, and which was, presumably, only the afterlife.

When the photographer went away, bubbling with fizzy youth, to write a whole book about her, Leocadia went up to her studio, unhaunted by the deaths of Nanice and Asra.

She stood among the canvases and considered. Possibly death did not matter. Possibly stupidity and cruelty, banality, and rheumatism (which even the best drugs could not quite dispel) did not count.

What counted, then?

Why, what we want. What we truly desire.

"Write," said Leocadia, "in the great fat tome of time. Real desire, of any sort, is what counts."

And when she was one hundred and five and a half, Leocadia was painting the Penguin Land in her studio, slowly, because her hand was stiff. When in the ice sculpture before her, beyond the picture, she caught an image.

It was of a girl—two girls, but one not long ago a child. And both had marmalade hair.

She heard their laughter like distant bells.

Leocadia imagined that behind her the wall had opened, and there lay heaven, with snow and flowers, a sea of golden wine, a penguin king and a queen in a crown of ice.

If she means it, the minx, she'll throw a snowball at me. Then I'll look round and it will be there, and I can go in.

And Leocadia would be young. And though it might not be forever, it would be, at least, for one long, shining day.

And then the snowball, which was warm as toast, struck her shoulder.